The Big Bag of Infinite Cats: A Cozy Mystery

An Infinite Cats Mystery, Volume 1

Adam Drake

Published by Adam Drake, 2018.

This is a work of fiction. Similarities to real people, places, or events are entirely coincidental.

THE BIG BAG OF INFINITE CATS: A COZY MYSTERY

First edition. August 21, 2018.

Copyright © 2018 Adam Drake.

ISBN: 979-8201687083

Written by Adam Drake.

The Big Bag of Infinite Cats
An Infinite Cats Cozy Mystery
Book 1
By
Adam Drake
Copyright © 2018
Adam Drake

Books By Adam Drake

Infinite Cats Cozy Mysteries
The Big Bag of Infinite Cats[1]
Magical Mischief[2]
The River's Dream[3]
Infinite Cats Cozy Bundles
Infinite Cats Books 1-3[4]
Kingdom
Kingdom Level One[5]
Kingdom Level Two[6]
Kingdom Level Three[7]
Kingdom Level Four[8]
Kingdom Level Five[9]
Kingdom Level Six[10]
Kingdom Level Seven[11]
Kingdom Books 1-4 Bundle[12]
Kingdom Books 5-7 Bundle[13]
Shadow For Hire

1. https://www.amazon.com/Big-Bag-Infinite-Cats-ebook/dp/B07D21ND58/

2. https://www.amazon.com/gp/product/B0CZ47YLJ6

3. https://www.amazon.com/gp/product/B0CXWRPRXC

4. https://www.amazon.com/dp/B0DC5C2PY5

5. http://www.amazon.com/dp/B076BBCRJM

6. http://www.amazon.com/dp/B076B7M1CK

7. http://www.amazon.com/dp/B0769XF3QV

8. http://www.amazon.com/dp/B078QLPB1M

9. http://www.amazon.com/dp/B0CSBBJBH5

10. http://www.amazon.com/dp/B0CSFS5H5S

11. http://www.amazon.com/dp/B0D57WT4JV

12. http://www.amazon.com/dp/B07D1FCX1P

13. https://www.amazon.com/Kingdom-LitRPG-Bundle-Books-Bundles-ebook/dp/
B0DT8QNX32

<u>Shadow Gambit</u>[14]
<u>Shadow Hunting</u>[15]
<u>Shadow Wars</u>[16]
<u>Shadow Blade</u>[17]
<u>Shadow For Hire Books 1-4 Bundle</u>[18]
<u>Other Titles</u>
<u>Mage Levels 1-5</u>[19]
<u>Bitch Berserker</u>[20]
<u>Escape To The Fringe</u>[21]
<u>The First Day</u>[22]

14. http://www.amazon.com/dp/B072BB4YMS

15. http://www.amazon.com/dp/B07258GTNG

16. http://www.amazon.com/dp/B0727WJ83W

17. http://www.amazon.com/dp/B071HH3VF1

18. http://www.amazon.com/dp/B07425ML3V

19. https://www.amazon.com/Mage-Levels-1-5-Adam-Drake-ebook/dp/B0DKWX78H1

20. http://www.amazon.com/dp/B07DBRXV4Z

21. https://www.amazon.com/Escape-Fringe-Science-Fiction-Adventure-ebook/dp/B093PB4SFJ/

22. https://www.amazon.com/First-Day-Total-Collapse-Book-ebook/dp/B08JKFX2HK/

The Big Bag of Infinite Cats

A Supernatural Cozy Mystery

A baffling mystery of ancient magic

When a strange case of a detective being turned to stone stumps local police, retired investigator Mayra Beeweather is asked to assist. One of her tools of the trade is a magical bag which contains an infinite number of cats. Very *special* cats – each with a unique ability to aid in her investigation.

Yet, even with their help, Mayra may not solve the case in time, for she may be the next victim turned to stone.

I sat on my favorite park bench, perusing the newspaper when someone said, "Excuse me, Miss Beeweather, but might you help me, please?"

Bleary-eyed from reading small print, I looked up at the speaker, and squinted against the morning sun. "Beg pardon?" I said.

It was Penny, a frazzled looking red headed woman, who stood before me on the cobblestone path. She looked concerned, hands rubbing together like frightened animals. "I'm afraid it's my son, Newlin, miss," Penny said. "He's got himself stuck up that tree."

I looked where she pointed.

Sure enough, at the edge of the glade, high up a thick oak, a small red headed boy straddled a branch. He clung to the trunk with both arms for dear life. He looked as frazzled as his mother.

Now, to a casual observer it might strike them as odd to ask for help in this endeavor from someone of my advanced years. Especially when a fair amount of climbing would be involved. But supposed limits of old age has nothing on ability.

"Well," I said, "He's good and stuck, now, isn't he?" I assessed the situation. "It appears he has made it up quite high, indeed."

"Yes, miss," Penny said, quick to agree.

"An ambitious little fellow," I said, and stood. Various creaks and pops betrayed my bones with the effort. I put the newspaper down on the bench and shouldered my satchel with care. "Well, let's see if help is in the offering, shall we?"

Happy, Penny nodded and we walked over to the base of the great oak. On closer inspection, I saw the child, his eyes red with tears, scrapes on his arms and elbows.

"Are you okay, lad?" I called up to him.

"Y-yes ma'am," the little boy sputtered.

I squinted at him. "Now, why would a smart little boy like yourself do something so silly as get stuck up a tree?"

The little boy scrunched his face with concern. This appeared to be more than a random adventure which resulted in his getting stuck.

I frowned a little, more for emphasis than anything close to anger. "You wouldn't have done this on purpose now? You saw me sitting over there and thought being saved might be fun?"

Penny held up her hands in alarm. "Oh, no Miss Beeweather. My lad wouldn't do such a thing. He likes exploring, is all. Like Kadmik the Adventurer."

"I like Kadmik," Newlin said.

I arched a suspicious brow at the two of them. "When Kadmik went exploring," I said, "he had an army at his side. Accompanied by your own legion of soldiers helps when you're stuck up a tree." I rummaged through my satchel.

"Kadmik tamed beasts and was the friend to giants!" the boy declared.

"Yes, yes," I said, feeling annoyed to hear distorted myths from a child. "I'm sure that's the version taught to you. Ah, here we are." I pulled out a tall knitting bag and set it on the ground.

I sensed the eyes of the woman and child on it, eager to see what happens next.

The knitting bag always got people's attention. Preceded by its reputation it had become an attraction. I wondered if I should charge a fee each time I brought it out. At least that would help pay for morning newspapers.

The top opening of the knitting bag was closed with a knobbed clasp. Much to my relief the clasp was brass. If it were wooden, there would be no rescue. At least not by me. The bag's fabric was of a dull gray wool embroidery, with no obvious design, and gave no hints as to its actual contents.

Suffice to mention this bag was not meant for knitting.

As I reached forward, I glanced at Penny and Newlin. Anticipation created wide eyed masks of their faces.

Fine, a copper piece each, I decided, and touched the clasp.

With only a light tap, the clasp snapped undone. Unaided, the knitting bag opened wide.

I have to admit. No matter how many times I've done this throughout the years, I still get excited at opening it. The hairs on my arms stood up on end.

The bag wiggled as if alive. In moments, the shaking intensified. Something was trying to climb out.

Then, from within, a small furry head emerged. The head turned, surveying the outside surroundings, and settled on me. A gorgeous white cat matched my wide-eyed gaze.

"Hello, there," I said. I did not move, nor made any effort to approach or touch this new arrival. I knew from experience there might be unwanted results.

"It's a cat, ma!" cried the boy.

"Hold still," Penny said. She looked at the cat with apprehension. Frightened, even. An almost universal reaction by most.

"Help," I said to the cat and pointed toward the little boy.

The cat looked from me and up at Newlin. It blinked several times. Its irises appeared composed of brightly colored rainbows with countless hues. Its thick fur was as white as the first winter snow.

As if finally deciding what to do, the cat hopped out of the bag. It paused, sat back on hind legs, and proceeded to clean a forepaw.

It had been several months since I'd seen a white cat emerge from the bag. I could not tell if this was the same one as that time. There was no way to be certain by quick observation.

But what this cat did would set it apart from any another.

I felt a strong sense of pride looking at it. A different cat with almost every summoning. All the same indefinable breed, but of varying colors. Each unique in their own way. An infinite number of them. And all a welcome sight.

"Is it going to save me now?" Newlin asked, his voice tinged with worry.

"Hush, now, child," I said. "Give her a moment."

Once the cat finished cleaning itself, it got down to business. With an almost imperious saunter, it strolled over to the tree and stopped right below the boy. It peered up at him. The distance that separated the two was twenty spans or more. If this did not work then a call to the fire department would be needed.

As we all stood by with bated breath, the cat tensed up as if ready to pounce. Its focus never wavered from the boy.

Then, the cat vanished with an audible pop.

Penny gasped, hands to her mouth.

My heart beat quickened, and up I looked.

The cat now sat on the tree branch, next to the little boy. It had somehow travelled the distance from the ground in an instant. Faster than a blink.

The boy craned his neck around to look at the cat with wide-eyed apprehension.

I said, "It's okay, child. She's going to help you."

The cat stood up and brushed against the boy. Even from a distance its purr could be heard.

"Is it going to -," Newlin said and both he and the cat were suddenly gone.

At that same moment, with another loud pop, both cat and child appeared on the ground, safe.

Penny gasped with relief, but when she rushed over to her child, she froze, uncertain what to do. The cat sat in the boy's lap rubbing against him.

Newlin giggled and stroked the creature's fur.

As if deciding its job finished, the cat jumped onto the grass and walked away.

Penny joined her child and scooped him into her arms. "Don't you ever do that again, young man! What would we have done if Miss Beeweather had not been here?"

I doubted any trees would have been climbed without my presence. Yet, with the child safe now, it didn't matter.

I watched the beautiful white cat trot across the ground straight back to the knitting bag. And, without a glance back at any of us, it leapt into the bag's opening and was gone in an instant. The opening closed on its own, and the clasp snapped shut. Now, instead of brass, the clasp was of a polished wood.

I exhaled my breath. Astounding. Simply astounding. Anytime I needed to open the bag was a moment an old woman like me looked forward too.

Penny held the boy tight and kissed him. "Thank you so much, Miss Beeweather. I apologize for bothering you."

With a curt nod I put the knitting bag back into the satchel and walked back to my seat. I hoped my manner indicated a repeat of this child's escapade would not be tolerated. But noticing how Newlin's eyes followed the satchel, I suspected he would be in need of aid again.

I returned to the bench and grabbed up my newspaper, intent on resuming my morning read.

Movement caught my eye.

A uniformed policeman walked up the path toward me and I instantly recognized him. Constable Fairfax. His bushy walrus mustache could make him identifiable even from a thousand paces. From his somber expression I knew this morning's distractions would be amplified.

"Good morning, Miss Beeweather," said Fairfax and tipped his cap as he approached to stand before me, his voice deep and somber.

"Good morning, Constable," I said. "Did you, by chance, bring me any biscuits?"

"Beg pardon, ma'am?"

"Biscuits? I have a strong craving for them this morning."

"I'm afraid not," Fairfax said, looking uncertain. "My apologies."

"Then I take it this interruption is not a social call?"

"No ma'am, it is not." The constable cleared his throat. "The Chief Constable is requesting your assistance on a matter."

"I see," I said. "What is it this time?" Assisting the Chief Constable had become a more frequent event than helping adventurous little boys. In many ways, they were almost one and the same.

"There has been a murder," Fairfax said. He delivered this line as if describing the cloudy weather.

I sighed and fingered my neglected newspaper. "I am retired, Constable."

"Yes, ma'am."

"Murder falls well under the purview of Detective Constable Radley Oswall. And he will not be retiring for many years. Am I correct?"

"Yes, ma'am. But - " Fairfax said before I interrupted him.

I said, "Is Oswall on vacation, perhaps? Or did he fall deep into his cups again?" I felt my annoyance growing. Oswall was a good detective but his vices had become greater than his sense of duty.

Fairfax's expression rippled with emotion. A rare and unusual event given his perpetual dourness.

This got my attention. "Fairfax," I said, concerned now. "What is it?"

"That's the thing ma'am," Fairfax managed. "It's Detective Oswall who was murdered."

<u>CHAPTER TWO</u>

We walked through the park to the spot on the road where Fairfax had parked his buggy. The vehicle was a sad looking contraption with dents and scrapes along its paneling, and little cracks in the windows. I plunked myself into the passenger seat which squeaked and rattled.

"It's the only vehicle issue available," Fairfax said by way of apology as he got behind the wheel.

"Has any new ones been issued to the Constabulary since I left?" I asked. The town council, notoriously stingy when it came to budgeting, seemed to make it a point that the Protection and Investigation services always suffered the most when it came to financing.

"No," Fairfax said, and frowned. The motion caused his thick mustache to bristle like an agitated porcupine. "Nothing."

I was stunned. "All these years?"

His embarrassed silence was answer enough.

I huffed, but did not prod. The political fighting between the town council and the impoverished police force was now legendary. Even throughout my tenure it never reached a point of resolve.

I shook my head. Why should this matter to me now? I'm retired.

Fairfax tried to start the buggy, but it refused to cooperate. After a few tries, and some grumbling from Fairfax, it sputtered to life. We pulled out into the street and drove toward the edge of town.

Through the passenger window I watched the trees of the park zip past. I did not want to be in this situation. Not again. But Oswall was dead...

"Tell me more, please," I said. "Where was he found?"

Eyes on the road, Fairfax said, "Under a bridge along Muddy Way. A couple found him early this morning."

I knew the area. "Why would they be walking along Muddy Way in the early morning? The place is devoid of anything of note. Other than trees, mud and the risk of being robbed by bandits."

"I don't know," he said with a shrug. "We can ask them."

"No, you can ask them," I said. "You are the acting detective now, after all. With Oswall gone, you are next in seniority."

Fairfax took a moment to digest this. He said, "I thought you would assist with the investigation."

"I said I would take a look, nothing more. If I can help with the initial survey, then I will. But I am through with detective work."

Quiet now, Fairfax gripped the wheel a little tighter.

"Oh, I'm sorry Fairfax," I said. "But I cannot let myself get dragged into another case. Not again."

Fairfax glanced at me, his expression unreadable. I sensed his frustration. From what I knew he only started his detective training and trial period. It would be a good year before he would earn a Detective Constable's badge.

I felt sorry for him. I did. By refusing to help I put him in a lurch. The pressure to solve Oswall's murder, or any murders, would be all his. But I refused to get involved any more. That part of my life was finished. Now I rescued stranded children, which suited me fine.

"I understand, ma'am," Fairfax said. "And I respect it. Thank you for coming, anyway."

Inspecting the murder scene was the most I wanted to do. I tried to not let a swell of guilt overcome me, but failed. This would not be easy.

"Here we are," Fairfax said, indicating the road ahead.

There were several police buggies parked along the road side, next to the entrance of a bridge. The bridge itself was of a stone construction from an era long gone. A rickety wooden roof covered its length and looked to be in severe disrepair.

Fairfax parked us next to the other buggies. I felt a fluttering of butterflies in my stomach. Whenever I arrived at a crime scene, murder or otherwise, it always gave me a shot of energy. I tried to ignore it.

When I exited the vehicle another constable approached me with a grin. "Miss Beeweather. Glad to see you're here. How are you doing these days?"

"Fit and fine, Constable Webster, thank you," I said. Better than Detective Oswall, I thought, then frowned. When had I become such a bitter old fool?

A man and woman skulked nearby in the shade of a tree and were talking with a constable who scribbled notes on a pad. The couple shot concerned glances in our direction.

"They are the ones who found Oswall?"

"Yes, ma'am," Webster said.

"They look nervous," I said.

Webster looked at them. "Yes, but I don't think they have the ability to have done it."

"Why is that, Constable?" First rule at the start of a murder investigation is that everyone is a suspect. Everyone.

"Only that I don't know who or what could have killed Oswall in such an... odd manner."

Intrigued now, I said, "Lead the way, please, if you will."

I followed the constables to the river embankment. From its edge, I looked down at the sluggish river rippling past. Its slate gray water reflected the morning sun.

"He's under there," Fairfax said, pointing toward the bank below the bridge. From this angle nothing appeared amiss.

As we climbed down the rocky embankment Fairfax offered me his hand. I declined with a polite smile and made it to the bottom on my own without tumbling fanny-over-teakettle.

We crossed the shadowed terminus of the bridge, and I spotted Detective Oswall.

I stopped, agog.

It was Oswall. He stood upright which, for a dead body, indicated something obviously strange. Cloaked in shadow, and facing away from me, he had one arm extended before him.

I took a few steps closer. Stock still, the man made no movement. The breeze here did not so much as disturb a hair on his head, nor did it ruffle his pullover coat.

As I drew up to him, I gasped in disbelief.

"He's been turned to stone!" I said, amazed.

"So it would appear," Fairfax said.

I looked closer, and nodded. Definitely Oswall, right done to the last detail. If I didn't know that he was solid stone I would have sworn he had been completely painted a rocky brownish color. Even his eyes, wide in shock, had been affected.

For several moments, I only stared at him. I knew him, I'd worked with him, and I helped train him. But now?

He was a statue. Caught in a pose of warding someone or something away. His other hand gripped the pistol at his hip, still holstered, and all stone.

"I have a strong dislike for these magic cases," Webster said, keeping his distance from Oswall.

"They can be challenging," Fairfax said. I sensed he disapproved of the younger constable a little. Then he said, "Oh, Chief Constable's direct order is that no one is to mention what has befallen Oswall. Not without his say so. Doesn't want to create a panic."

I nodded, then said, "Someone caught him off guard," noting Oswall's stance.

"Snuck up on him," Webster said.

I shook my head and tried to figure the angle of Oswall's eyes. "It doesn't appear so. See how he is facing directly ahead. Not toward the edge of the bridge foundation where a person might jump out. It looks like he was perhaps speaking with someone. Or someone approached him from along the river bank."

The two constables mumbled their agreement.

I blinked out of my thoughts and realized I had forgotten to ask the obvious. "We are certain this is Oswall, yes? Not a carved statue placed here as a joke? Oswall is not at home sick in bed while we fiddle about in the mud?"

"Yes, ma'am," Fairfax said. "I went to speak with his wife just before coming to you. She'd been beside herself with worry as Oswall had not returned home last night, or this morning. She thought he was on an extended stake out, but upon seeing me coming up the walk she started to cry." He frowned.

I nodded. To tell a person that a loved one was dead had always been the worst part of working this job.

I wanted to ask Fairfax how he explained Oswall's manner of death to his wife, but refrained. Not my affair. Instead, I asked, "When was the last time anyone saw him?"

Webster said, "Maginhart said he left the Constabulary shortly after seven last night, as best he can remember."

"His wife last saw him yesterday morning, before leaving for work," said Fairfax.

My eyes roamed up and down Oswall's rocky figure. One hand on his pistol, the other held out in front of him, its palm up and flat as if trying to deflect something. Eyes wide in fear? Shock? Horror?

I noticed a thick little spiral bound note pad sticking out of the exposed inside jacket pocket of his coat. It, too, was complete stone.

"There's his case book."

"Yes," Fairfax said. "Won't be much help to us now, unfortunately."

That was an understatement. As a detective worked a case, he scribbled notes in a notebook which was almost always on his person. If Oswall met someone here, which is how it appeared, he might have written the name in his case book.

Struck with a thought, I looked at Oswall's shoes. The stone soles of them did not appear to be fused with muddy ground beneath. Whatever occurred here only affected Oswall.

Then I saw something else and knelt closer.

"What is it?" Fairfax said.

"Look," I said and pointed. "See how the mud under his feet is pushed outward?" A little trough of mud ringed the base of both shoes.

"Perhaps he's slowly sliding into the river?" Webster offered.

"No," I said. "See how the cleared area extends to both sides of him, toward the river and then the opposite direction."

"Someone moved him," said Fairfax and scowled.

"Heavy that," Webster said.

"Too much for whomever tried to push him," I said. Oswall was a husky fellow, almost portly. Before he was heavy, now he was almost immovable.

I looked around the area in front of Oswall, in the direction he was looking. The mud and rock debris here made it impossible to see footprints.

"We did a sweep," Fairfax said as he watched me inspecting the muddy ground. "The boys did a thorough job."

"That couple sullied the crime scene when they found him. Walking about and all," Webster said.

"I am aware," I said. I still looked. Once I reached the far side of the bridge the ground became too rocky.

There had to be something. I sensed it. I took a moment to glance inside my satchel. The knitting bag's clasp remained wooden. No help there.

The river chuckled at me while it coursed along.

Webster asked Fairfax, "How are we going to move him, anyway? Just from looking at him I'd guess he must be as heavy as a plow horse."

"We'll get the truck so to keep him covered," Fairfax said, frustration growing in his voice.

I looked toward the underside of the bridge; a thick, stone laced wall. I thought I caught the glint of something.

"Yes, but then what? Push him onto it somehow? Would take all the constables in the force to do that. Maybe more," Webster said.

I approached the wall. Something was there, drawn on its surface.

"That is a matter of concern for later," Fairfax said. "Right now is the investigation."

Webster wouldn't let it go. "We could tie ropes to him, then drag him behind the truck. That might work."

Fairfax ground his teeth in frustration, but I would not be distracted. I came up on the drawing. No, not a drawing. An engraving.

It looked at first glance to be just a set of long squiggly lines running up and down on the surface of a flat stone. By squinting at it I made out a figure. A long bulbous head, with a half dozen tentacles dangling below it.

A squid.

"There will be no dragging of constables while I'm in charge, understand?" Fairfax said.

"Maybe we can push him with the truck," Webster said, still thinking over the dilemma.

"Gentlemen," I said with mild exasperation. "Did you notice this?"

The two constables walked closer.

"Yes," Webster said. "Noted and disregarded."

"How so?" I asked with genuine surprise. "This might be important."

"Well, it's just a bit of graffiti," Webster said. "That sort of thing is everywhere now."

"Everywhere? Graffiti or this specific image?" I asked.

Webster shrugged. "Both, really." He sensed my annoyance. "I'll add it to my report, though." He walked away, making a show of writing in his own case book, trying to get a safe distance from me.

I sighed then held my hand over the etching without touching it and felt a faint tingling sensation against my palm.

"Magic?" Fairfax asked.

"Yes. Someone spelled this into place," I said, withdrawing my hand to fish through my satchel. "Also, see how clean the area is around it? This was created recently. Maybe at the time of the attack."

"Those have been appearing all around town," Fairfax said, peering at the squid image. "No idea what it could mean. Do you?"

I found what I was looking for and pulled out a long piece of paper and a charcoal pencil. On occasion, an old bird like me took to drawing the locals strolling through the park. I was terrible at it.

"No, I don't. Here, hold this up, will you?" I said. Fairfax pressed the paper against the stone and I ran the pencil across it, capturing the squid image.

Finished, I rolled the paper up and put it back in my satchel.

"Did anyone find his buggy?" I asked.

"No, we haven't. I have constables searching further down the road, past the bridge, and another down the river. There's an old dirt lane running along it from here."

"Well, he had to arrive at this spot somehow. Either someone dropped him off, which I seriously doubt, or someone took his buggy after he was... stoned."

"It was a police vehicle so I don't think they would drive it about on a lark," Fairfax said.

I nodded, hands on my hips. "Okay, this should do for the moment. Now, let's go talk to our prime suspects."

Fairfax raised his eyebrows. "Prime suspects? Those two mud people?"

As we walked past Oswall a pang of sadness struck me. He had been a good man, overall.

"Until you can delve into Oswall's case files, those mud people are the only suspects you have."

<u>CHAPTER THREE</u>

We climbed back up the embankment and walked to the buggies. Overhead, the morning sun crawled up the blue sky and I realized Oswall would never witness another sunrise ever again.

The couple were still in their shady spot, only now they appeared to be more annoyed than nervous. As he smoked a cigarette, the man tried to blow rings at his companion. When we approached they jumped to attention as if at a military inspection.

"Good morning," I said.

They both mumbled a good morning in return, and I got a better assessment of them. The woman was short and stout, hard looking. A tough life no doubt made her appear far older than she was. Dirt and filth etched every wrinkle on her face and hands. She wore a coat, which was too small for her plump figure, and clutched a tiny old purse in front of her.

The man wore a baggy patchwork overcoat, pea green trousers which did nothing to conceal his mismatched socks, and a beaten up cap. He was just as grimy as she was.

Fairfax was quiet so I simply jumped into questioning. "May I ask your names, please?" I said.

The man spoke. "I'm Malwin Amata and this here is my sister, Gescha."

"And you found this man this morning, correct?"

"Yeah, that's right."

"And what was your business down here at the river at such an early hour?"

Malwin looked a little flustered at the question. "Well, our business here is our own, ain't it? What business is that of yours?"

"Malwin, be polite with the lady," Gescha said.

Her brother crossed his arms and curled a lip. "I already spoke to that other constable over there. Why don't you go get what I said from him, eh?"

I kept my expression neutral, but inwardly I sighed.

Fairfax leaned in and said, "Just answer the questions, now. You don't want any trouble."

Gescha punched her brother in the shoulder. "We want to talk, right?" she said to him and he scowled.

I tried a different tactic. "We want to clear you as suspects so you folks can be on your way."

This had the desired effect. Malwin uncrossed his arms and his scowl vanished.

"Suspect?" he said with alarm. "We ain't no suspects, just found him is all. We had no hand in whatever it was that happened to him."

I gave him a slight smile. "And what were you two doing here?"

Malwin scratched his stubbly chin. "Looking for things that wash up along the riverside. Bits and pieces of things. Something to sell. You never know what the river gives up on occasion. Especially for someone who's hard on his luck."

From the state of these two I knew his reason was most likely plausible. Hard times abound. But it had always been that way. People were forced to do anything to make a few copper bits. Scavenging was the most common.

"What happened when you found him?" I said.

Malwin blinked wide eyed a few times as if trying to manifest the event from his memory. "We were following the river from the Hearts district, since about four this morning. Didn't find anything worth our time and effort. So, if nothing is found at one part of it, you gotta keep walking along until you do. Took some two hours before we ended up here. I was telling Gescha that maybe we should just turn back or we'll be stuck out in the woods at night fall."

"He gives up so easily," Gescha said.

Malwin glared at her. "Do not!"

Gescha frowned, shaking her head, then said, "Put a drink in his hand and he'll be in the cups all day and night. But try to make him earn the money for those drinks, even for a little while, and he collapses like wet parchment."

"That's not true at all, and you know it!"

I interjected before things got out of hand. "So what time was it when you arrived at this bridge?"

"Probably six, I'd say. Not much later than that."

"And what happened?"

Again, Malwin's eyes fluttered. "We found him is what happened. Under the bridge there. At first I thought it was a bandit skulking in the shadows looking to rob fine folks, such as ourselves. I called out to him not to try anything funny or he'd regret it!"

"No you didn't," Gescha said. "You told me to go and look under the bridge. See who was there. Brave man that you are."

Quick to cut off Malwin's anger, I asked, "Was there anyone else around, besides you two?"

"Nah," Malwin said. "No one. Just us two. Strangest thing, ain't it? Man like that now all stone like. I was telling Gescha here that it could only be great magic which could do that to a person. Didn't I?"

Gescha nodded. "Great magic. Very special. Thought something as special as a stone man should be noted to the police."

This was what had me wondering since the moment I saw them. These types of folk did their utmost to avoid authorities.

"Now why did you two feel compelled to report it?"

Gescha regarded me with surprise at the question. "Well, for the reward, of course."

"Reward?"

"Yeah, reward. There has to be one when a stone man is found."

I heard Fairfax grinding his teeth.

"There is no reward, Miss Amata. There never was."

The two of them looked horrified.

"No reward?" Malwin said. "It's special, ain't it? You can't fool me that it isn't. A stone man has gotta be worth something to someone. Maybe we should sell it."

Fairfax had reached the end of his rope and said, "There is no reward, and that stone man is not yours to claim."

"I doubt that," Malwin said, giving a shrewd look. "We found him. We should be able to keep him. Sell him to the highest bidder. Scavenger's rights!"

Now I sighed. "When you two found him, you thought you could sell him. But when you tried to move him, to haul him away to one of the black markets, you found he was too heavy. Correct?"

"Well, yeah," Gescha said.

"And since he was too heavy to move you figured you might get a reward which is why you flagged down a police buggy. Correct?"

"Yeah," Malwin said. He looked as confused as his sister. They both realized now they could never claim Oswall's stone body.

I then pulled out the paper with the etching on it and presented to them. "This was on the wall next to the body. Did either of you make this?"

They both looked at it, bewildered.

"No, we didn't," Gescha said. "What's that supposed to be anyway? A fish?"

"Nah, it's a dog," Malwin said. "See the tail there."

I frowned and put the paper back into my satchel. There was nothing more to ask.

"I would like to thank you for informing us of the stone man," I said. "The constable has your details and we will be in touch if we have further questions. Good day to you."

I turned and walked away. Fairfax stepped in front of the siblings before they could say any more, shooing them off.

I found my temper had been rising throughout the conversation. Not a trait a detective should possess if an investigation was to proceed. When did I get this way? I had always been professional during my time at work. But now?

Standing on the embankment and watching the river, I placed my hand into my satchel and caressed the knitting bag. Its texture soothed me.

A constable stood near the underside of the bridge, guarding poor Oswall's stone corpse. The detective deserved better than this. At least he died by a river. I wondered how I would die and if there would be a river nearby.

Fairfax appeared at my side. "What do you think?"

"Of those two? I think I'd eat my purse if they had the wherewithal to perform greater magic on Oswall, and then be dumb enough to inform the police about it."

Fairfax chuckled. A pleasant noise. "True. But could they have been involved?"

I shook my head. "They gave me no indication of anything like that. All they really did was sully the crime scene trying to move him. That explains the flattened mud at Oswall's feet. And good luck having them not mentioning this to anyone. They're off to spread the word of their grand discovery."

"Doubt anyone would believe them. Anyways, we can now cross off our only prime suspects," he said with mild humor.

I looked at him. Intelligent and duty bound, he would solve this case on his own and without an old woman's aid.

Might as well get this over with. I cleared my throat. "My assessment, Constable, is that this case is dangerous. Too dangerous, to be honest. Someone is out there, right now, with the ability to turn people to stone. A horrible magic if I ever heard of one. And catching the culprit will be very risky."

Fairfax frowned.

I continued, ignoring his disappointment. "I would start with whatever is on Oswall's desk, at the moment. That might give you a lead or two. But I believe you will find additional support is required."

"Not from a retired detective." Fairfax said it as a statement.

I sighed. "Get help from the Capital Constabulary. They may find this warrants a larger investigation than our local one can manage. That would be my recommendation. I'm sorry, but that is all I can offer you."

I looked away, not wanting to see his eyes. Home called for me. My only duties for the remainder of the day were crawling into bed and having a nice long nap. But would I dream of cats or stone men?

Fairfax nodded. "I understand. And I appreciate you coming here. Shall I take you home now?"

I was about to answer when a brilliant white car pulled off the road and parked next to where we stood. It lurched to a stop, kicking up dust and dirt into our eyes. This was one of the more expensive model of buggies, and usually could only be found in the Capital. The gaudy thing looked like a beached whale on wheels.

"It's the Mayor," Fairfax coughed out, swiping dust away from his face.

A fat little man jumped out of the passenger's side. He was bald, save for a pathetic wisp of a comb-over, and had a razor thin line of a mustache that edged his upper lip. Looking about with beady eyes he settled on me and scowled.

As the fat man marched over to us another man, this one tall and thin, emerged from the driver's side and hurried to catch up with his shorter companion.

"What is going on here?" the little fat man said.

"Oh, Sigwald," I said with maudlin tones. "Always a pleasure."

"That is Mayor Archambault to you, Mayra," Sigwald said. "What are you doing here?" He looked to Fairfax. "Why is she here? She is no longer a part of the force."

"She is here as a consultant," Fairfax said, evenly. "At the Chief Constable's express invitation."

Around us the other constables watched, but shrewdly kept a distance.

"Oh, that is wonderful isn't it?" Sigwald nearly spat. He looked at me. "Don't you think this case would be better suited in the hands of active duty investigators?"

"I wanted to see for myself -", I said but he interrupted.

"Wanted to see what? How a murder investigation is properly conducted?" He glared at Fairfax. "Will you be charging admission next? Hmm? Let the local children have a look at the body for a copper piece?"

"Miss Beeweather has the best case clearance rate in the history of the -", Fairfax said, but Sigwald wouldn't let him finish.

"Unprofessional is what it is!" Sigwald said.

"Most unprofessional," parroted the tall skinny man with a hook nose hovering behind Sigwald. He had an unseemly birthmark under his left eye. It was Davlon Blythe, the mayor's assistant and perpetual sycophant.

"And she is retired! Am I correct? She should not be here at all. In any capacity," Sigwald said.

"That is for the Chief Constable to decide," Fairfax said.

Sigwald barked a laugh. "The Chief Constable, eh? Well, we'll see what he thinks once I bring this to the Town Council's attention. That might clear his head of any notion of bringing Mayra into an investigation. And her little... circus."

The last was said with a hateful glance at my satchel.

Neither Fairfax nor I said anything in response. There was no point. It would only encourage Sigwald to make more of a spectacle.

When Sigwald realized we wouldn't cater to his tantrum, he whirled around and pointed at the nearest constable. "You, there! Take me to this poor fellow's body. I want to see for myself."

The unfortunate constable looked to Fairfax, who begrudged a nod.

We watched as Sigwald disappeared over the river embankment with his assistant and a cluster of frightened constables in his wake.

"What an unpleasant little man," I said.

Fairfax snorted and said, "Well, you did have two of his business partners thrown in prison for a good long time."

I placed a hand on the knitting bag within the satchel and smiled at Fairfax. "Oh, yes. There was that. I had forgotten."

"He hasn't," Fairfax said.

Nor would he ever. I thought about Sigwald and the terror he induced in everyone around him. The little man flared up my temper good and hot. Though putting his partners away had been a highlight of my career, there had been nothing to directly link Sigwald to their crimes. Yet even the stink of corruption didn't put a dent in Sigwald's campaign to get reelected as Mayor.

Still, I found I enjoyed the thought of making Sigwald annoyed. Maybe I would like to make him even more annoyed.

"Shall I take you home now, miss?" Fairfax said, motioning toward his buggy.

"No," I said. "That won't be necessary."

Fairfax looked at me in surprise.

"Let us have a gander at Oswall's desk," I said with a grin.

CHAPTER FOUR

The Constabulary looked the same as when I last visited. Not that I expected any great change. The building had been in use by the Protection Services for at least a century. Perhaps I feared the neglect of the Town Council toward the department had caused the place to collapse out of sheer ambivalence. I was relieved to see it had not.

We pulled around the back and onto a gated lot. There were only two other buggies parked there.

"Everyone is on scene or doing their patrols," Fairfax said as he parked nearest to the building's rear door.

"Of course," I said. I felt for Fairfax. He was a true sworn protector and always made excuses when something lacking of Protection Services became obvious.

No doubt he made constant excuses.

I exited the buggy, satchel clutched close to my side and looked at the place. Old and perfunctory. Like me. I smiled at my own dull humor.

Fairfax noticed and arched a questioning brow as he opened the Constabulary's back door. "Care to share the joke?"

A shook my head. "No, Fairfax. Just a bit of gas." This time I chuckled and feared Fairfax thought I'd lost my mind.

Inside, the tiled floor gleamed brightly, reflecting the sunlight which passed through huge bay windows.

I squinted, surprised. "This is new," I said.

"Chief Constable fought hard for it to get done but the Council refused to approve any funds. In the end, the Chief called on a few favors and finished it a few weeks ago."

I could hear a mix of pride and frustration in his voice. I said no more.

The Sergeant Constable stood at a counter in front of the wide open doorway which led into the main room of the Constabulary. His job was to field queries which came through and direct them accordingly.

He beamed once he spotted me.

"Detective Beeweather! You are a welcome sight. How have you been, if I may enquire?"

"Still alive, Sergeant Maginhart. But please, no Detective, just Miss Beeweather," I said, feeling a flush across my cheeks. Gannon Maginhart was one of the longest serving constables in the service. And he was quite handsome, too.

Gannon grinned. "Of course. Miss it is." I took pleasure in noticing he did not glance at my satchel. Either he didn't care or made an effort to not show it. Regardless, I appreciated the gesture.

Gannon held a pen over the large log book in front of him. "Should I write you down as Acting Detective, then?"

Fairfax answered for me. "Please put her as a consultant, will you Maginhart?" He knew another title might cause a dust up with a review board.

"Very well," Sergeant Maginhart said, and made a scribble on the thick parchment.

I spotted a tin of biscuits on Maginhart's desk. "May I?" I asked.

"Please, help yourself."

I snatched up a biscuit and made a point of giving Fairfax a smug look while I chewed it down.

"Chief back, yet?" Fairfax asked, trying to ignore me.

"No. He went back to the scene," Maginhart said, and a sad expression crossed his handsome face.

"Did Oswall make any official log entries in the last few days?" I asked.

Maginhart shook his head. "I already checked. Nothing for over three months, and that time was to log a sick day. To be honest, I think it was to recover from a hangover."

I frowned. "Okay, thank you."

We passed through into the inner sanctum. As I looked around I was hit with a wave of memories.

The huge room, or the 'kennel', as the constables liked to refer to it, was lined with large windows. Twelve desks, in three rows, made up most of the decorum. Cabinets, filled with case files and paperwork, took up every available space. Books and file folders were piled everywhere, some threatening to spill over at the slightest touch. Several doorways were at the back leading to a small kitchen area, and the Chief Constable's office. A door to the armory was closed and locked.

Rock lights, now dark, hung over each desk from the high ceiling. More rock lights protruded at intervals along the wall.

The place smelled of must and paper and old overcoats. I often thought of the Constabulary as a lair for justice. Cases were launched from here and suspects pursued.

I worked here many years. Often spending more time under these rock lights than the ones in my own house.

As much as I did not want to admit it, this had been my home for a very long time.

I must have been standing in a daze before realizing Fairfax was speaking to me.

"Are you all right?" he asked.

I smiled and blinked away the start of a tear. "Yes. Yes, of course." I cleared my throat. "Is he still at the same desk?"

"Yes, last one on the right."

We walked to it and I glanced at each desk. Case files, photographs, paper, mugs half filled with morning tea. Once the call came in that Radley had been found everyone left in a hurry.

Oswall's desk looked different than the rest. It was very clean, devoid of any clutter. Several dip pens in a small cup, a fat little ink bottle, several reference books lined up neat on one corner, and a small hunched rock light. A wide ink blotter took up most of the desk space and tucked within its edge folder were two pieces of paper.

I looked around in mild surprise. "Where are his case files? They should be here." Each constable had a stack of active case files on their desk. Oswall, as the Constabulary's only active detective, was assigned the high-ticket items; high profile robberies and murders.

Fairfax thought a moment and said, "The Chief must have been looking at them. I'll see." He vanished into the Chief's office.

I picked up one of the papers stuck in the blotter. I recognized Oswall's loopy scrawl across one side of it. 'Hubertus – useless'. The other side was a large question mark.

The name Hubertus derived from the north-eastern region but was too common to pin down to one individual.

I took the other piece of paper and discovered it to be a business card. Rousset's Tomes & Books of Rarity, Misael Rousset Owner & Proprietor. The address was on a street off Stage Court, near the center of town. On the back of the card in Oswall's writing was a name, underlined: Elicia Ipthorn.

Fairfax emerged from the Chief's office with a stack of folders. "Here they are," he said as he set them down on the desk.

I counted them. Fourteen. "This was his active case load?" I asked, a little perplexed. That was an absurd amount to be given to a single detective. During my tenure there would be half as much, at most.

Fairfax shrugged. "Lots of crime recently, and not enough manpower."

I sighed and regarded the pile. "Let's have a quick check through these and see what stands out." We split them between us, flipping through each. We stood while reading. Neither one of us wanted to sit in Oswall's chair. It didn't feel proper.

As we read, constables trickled into the room. All either offered a warm greeting or gave a polite nod. Aware of our assignment, they left us to our task.

After three quarters of an hour, we finished. Oswall's case load composed of four murder cases, six armed robberies and four burglaries of note. Nothing jumped out to either of us as something that would result in Oswall being turned to stone.

"Well," Fairfax said, looking a tad overwhelmed. "This is going to take considerable time."

"That is the conundrum, isn't it?" I said. "At first glance, there is nothing here that tells us that investigating any of these cases got him killed. It could be someone from an older case, from years ago. Or it might be someone who isn't even related to any case, whatsoever. An old enemy from his past, perhaps?"

I sighed and Fairfax chewed at his bottom lip in thought.

On a hunch, I glanced inside my satchel. The knitting bag's brass clasp gleamed at me.

"I think we may get a lead," I said.

"We might?" Fairfax asked.

I grabbed the folders and fanned them across the tiled floor in two rows. Then I placed the satchel on Oswall's chair and opened it wide enough to expose the knitting bag.

Fairfax took a step back.

I chuckled. "You've seen me do this many times before, Fairfax. No need to worry."

"Yes, well, it's something that one never quite gets used to, eh?"

"True", I said, and touched the clasp with a finger.

The knitting bag shook and yawned open. After a few moments, the head of a cat emerged. It was silver this time, the same color as the coins in my purse. With multicolored eyes, it regarded me.

I bent over and pointed at the files on the floor. "Which folder will lead to Oswall's killer."

The cat did not move, nor did it blink. It continued to stare at me with multicolored eyes.

Waiting without further reaction, I tried again. Sometimes I needed to be more specific.

"Is there a case here that may lead to Detective Radley Oswall's attacker?"

To my relief the silver cat blinked and turned to look at the folders. Then it leapt out of the bag and gracefully landed on the floor. Again, this cat was the same breed as the others, fluffy with a wide tail.

It padded straight to one of the folders, turned around to face me, and sat on it.

"It appears we have a lead after all," Fairfax said with a slight smile.

"Indeed," I said.

The silver cat stood and walked back to the chair. It jumped into the knitting bag and vanished. The clasp snapped shut and became wooden once more.

I picked the folder up, and with Fairfax looking over my shoulder, read it.

The date on at the top of the first page showed the case was initiated on July fourteenth, three days prior.

It was a burglary at the High Garden Museum. The Head Curator, Aubert Othmar, reported several items missing from their vault, about twenty in all. Each one had an odd sounding name: Geggor's Tacticar, The Mullock, Brambles of Obsidian, etc.

The next sheet contained Oswall's notes of the crime scene, along with a black-and-white photograph of an open vault. The vault was still full of items, most wrapped and tagged. The stolen objects had been stored in a small locked trunk within, and the trunk was missing. Nothing else was taken from the museum.

Following procedure Oswall examined every door, window and obvious entryway, but found nothing amiss.

He then took the next step and interviewed the museum staff. There were eight individuals listed with scribbles by each name. No, no, no, maybe, nervous, pretty. By the curator's name, he had written, snob.

But the last name caught my attention: Winimar Hubertus. But Oswall had only written 'Night Caretaker' beside it.

"Well, now. We may have something," I said to Fairfax. I showed him the piece of paper from the blotter with the name Hubertus on it.

"A useless night caretaker, eh?" Fairfax said, ruminating.

"Is there any other kind?" I said.

The folder contained nothing else of note except empty forms which were to be filled in as the case progressed.

"Not much here," I said. "No details about the time of the burglary or the circumstances around it. He must not have gotten around to adding them yet."

"Whatever progress he made is in that notebook in his pocket."

"So," I said. "We need to retrace his movements and see what can be found. At least now we know where to start."

"And that is?"

I put the business card and piece of paper into the purse within my satchel, then held up the case file.

"Let's take a trip to the museum."

CHAPTER FIVE

The High Garden Museum was on a grassy plot of land at the west side of town. A huge building, it was several stories tall and made of flat gray brick rock. It had been a supply warehouse during the last great war, but now served a much more useful purpose.

Several horse drawn carriages and auto buggies were waiting at its front entrance, and that is where Fairfax parked.

I eyed the building, then withdrew a small pistol from my satchel and checked it was loaded.

Fairfax arched a brow. "Expecting trouble already?"

I gave Fairfax a point for not asking if I always carried it around. With such a long and successful career of throwing criminals in jail, the odds only increased that, even after many years, one of them may seek revenge.

With the pistol back in the satchel, I said, "I always expect trouble as a matter of course. But if that cat is right, whoever is responsible for Oswall's death is here. Or associated with it in some way. Best be prepared."

"Are those cats always correct?"

The question gave me pause. No, not always, I thought.

To Fairfax, I said, "Think of them as giving us a nudge in the right direction."

"If a nudge gets us Oswall's killer, I'm all for it," Fairfax said, and patted his holstered pistol with a grin.

We left the buggy and ascended the wide stairs to the entrance. Large columns lined either side and cast shadows across our path. I wondered at the cost of the place.

Cresting the top step we found the huge double doors of the front entrance closed. A stand in front had a sign which read 'Closed for the day. Will be open tomorrow promptly at 9 a.m.'.

"Well, this isn't helpful," Fairfax said.

I noticed a bell rope in a nook next to the doors and pulled it. From within could be heard the faint sound of chimes. We waited.

A man pushing a broom rounded one corner of the building. He wore a simple brown janitor's uniform with a flat hat. Upon seeing us he approached. "Ain't no one inside now," the man said.

"We're here to see the Curator," said Fairfax. "Is he around?"

The janitor leaned on his broom and pushed up his cap. "Sorry, Mister Othmar is in the Capital. Should be back by airship some time around afternoon tea."

"Capital?" I said.

"Yeah," said the janitor. "Got himself in a spot of trouble with the central museum there."

"What kind of trouble?" I said.

"His big bosses wanted to rake him over hot coals on account of the burglary," he said. Then he looked about and leaned closer. "If you ask me, it would do Mister Othmar good to have a talking to from his betters."

"Why is that?" I said.

"Well, he's a bit of snob, is all," the janitor said. "Needs to be taken down a peg or two. But you didn't hear that from me."

"Not to worry," I said. "We wanted to talk to him about the burglary. Were you here when it happened, by chance?"

The janitor's eyebrows shot up and disappeared beneath the rim of his cap. "Me? No, not at all. Happened at night. I was home in bed then, I was. You can ask my missus if you don't believe me. And that's what I told that detective fellow when he was here."

I offered a warm smile. "Are there any other employees here that we can speak with?"

He shook his head. "No ma'am. Everyone's at home or getting into their drink. Just me here, unfortunately. Could use a drink myself."

Fairfax asked, "Where can we find Winimar Hubertus? Do you know where he lives?"

Again, the janitor looked surprised. "The night caretaker? Didn't the detective tell you? Hubertus is still laid up in the hospital, last I heard. Doubtful he's recovered so soon."

Now it was my turn to be surprised. "Hospital? Was he hurt during the burglary?"

"Nah, not hurt. Not really," the janitor said. "He was asleep when Mister Othmar opened the doors in the morning. Sprawled out on the floor like a drunk soldier after the Victory Day celebrations. But it turned out he wasn't drunk at all. Heard he was spelled to sleep. Been that way close to three or four days now."

I glanced at Fairfax. It would have been nice to have that little detail in the report. To the janitor, I said, "He's at the Primary Hospital, I presume?"

"Yeah, that's the only one with a Warding Master who can work the spell outta him."

I nodded and said, "Very good. We will go see if the poor man is awake then. If you would be so kind as to inform Mister Othmar that we will call on him later?"

"Of course, Miss," the janitor said.

After giving him our names we returned to the buggy. Once inside, Fairfax said, "Spelled asleep? That's peculiar."

"And getting turned to stone is less peculiar?" I said.

"No, not what I meant," he said, scratching his bushy mustache. "Why would this Hubertus be put to sleep, but Oswall turned to stone?"

"True," I said. Then it hit me. "Unless we are dealing with two culprits working together."

Fairfax gave me a look. "Or we have two separate and unrelated cases. You sure those cats of yours can be trusted not to lead us astray?"

I did not point out Fairfax's unintentional pun. "They have given us our only lead. Or do you prefer to go back to the office and pick a case folder at random?"

Fairfax sighed and looked apologetic. "I don't mean to be gruff, Mayra. Just concerned we may well be wasting our time." He started the buggy and pulled out into the street.

It was then I realized two things. I'd moved a protective hand over the knitting bag while we spoke, and Fairfax had called me Mayra for the first time.

CHAPTER SIX

The Primary Hospital was of the same dull architecture as the museum, but much bigger with two wide wings and towered over four stories.

We parked out front and went in. A harried nurse directed us to the floor Winimar's room was located. I found the stairs too steep for a hospital, or I was just getting too old to climb them.

His room was at the furthest end, and as we approached the sound of voices could be heard. "Ain't right is what I'm saying," said a woman. "He can't just do that to you. Not after what you've been through."

A man answered. "Don't worry about it. I'll get Blythe to smooth it out, okay?"

To Fairfax, I said, "He's awake?" Fairfax shrugged. We moved to stand in the open doorway.

Inside, a man was lying in a small bed, the covers pulled up to his chest, and wearing a hospital gown tied at his neck.

Beside him, a short blonde woman sat on a stool. She was blue, or at least everything she wore was. Sky blue blouse, sky blue skirt, sky blue hat. Even her little purse was the same sky blue.

Both of them looked up at us in surprise.

"Beg your pardon, but is this the room of Winimar Hubertus?" I asked.

Both of them stared at us for a few seconds, neither speaking. As if trying to decide if they should answer.

The man cleared his throat. "I'm Winimar Hubertus. Might I ask who you are?"

I stepped into the little room. Fairfax stood in the doorway, blocking it while trying not to look like that was his intent.

35

"Mister Hubertus. My name is Mayra Beeweather, and this is Constable Fairfax. We were wondering if we could ask you a few questions."

"Well, I think -," Hubertus said before the woman in blue interrupted.

"Don't say nothing without a lawyer present, Win," she said and glared at Fairfax. "I don't like the looks of that one."

Winimar pulled himself up into a sitting position and said, "Why not? I've done nothing wrong. Can't hurt to speak with these fine police folk, now can it?" He gave me an inquisitive look. "You are police aren't you?"

Inwardly, I sighed. "Yes, I am the Acting Detective for this case." If Fairfax wasn't playing his role, he would have grinned.

The blue woman looked me over. "Acting, eh? What happened to the other detective that came round before? Oswall was it? He got himself fired for drinking on the job?" She turned to Winimar and said, "That man stank of whiskey and chips. You would have gotten along with him."

Winimar sighed, "Pasha, please. That is not called for."

I considered the response. If I mentioned that Oswall was dead, these two would become even more alarmed and clam up shut. Then I'd have to wait to speak with Winimar through a lawyer. There was no time for such nonsense.

"Detective Oswall is no longer on the case. I've taken over." To the blue lady, I said, "Your name is Pasha, is it?"

She frowned at me. "That's right. Pasha Hubertus. His wife. Third, actually. And he won't be needing for another wife after me. Ain't that right, Win?"

Winimar rolled his eyes. He said, "Is this about my being spelled? I woke up just a few hours ago. Slept all these days! Bit of a farce that."

"Yes. I understand that was what happened," I said and removed paper and a pencil from my satchel to take notes. "Could you tell us what happened that night? If you can remember."

"Oh, I remember," Winimar said. "Was making my rounds as usual. One circuit of the museum at the top and bottom of each hour. Every hour from nine at night until six in the morning until Mister Othmar opens the front doors."

"They don't pay him enough for that kind of boring work," Pasha said. "Can make someone go crazy walking in circles all night."

I wanted to keep Winimar talking. "Then what happened?"

"Well, I was making my rounds at about half past midnight and I needed to take a quick break. I walked to the lavatory which is between the Third and Fourth Era war displays. And as I rounded the corner to head down the hall, something caught my eye."

"They should have given you a pistol, is what they should have done," interrupted Pasha. She looked agitated.

"I don't need no pistol," Winimar said to her. "If there's any trouble I just pull an alarm and run like a Mudhump caught digging through the trash. If I had a pistol I'd probably just shoot myself in the foot."

Again, I redirected Winimar. "Something caught your eye?"

"Right. I looked over at the wax figure of General Tykish on his horse. And there was movement behind the General. Like a shadow or something."

Pasha said, "It's a good display, that. Even though Tykish messed it up and lost the battle, the display is quite pleasing to look at."

"A shadow?" I said to Winimar.

"Yeah. So I stopped and yelled 'Who goes there?' My heart was thumping right mad in my chest. I might be the night caretaker but I ain't no hero like Kadmik the Adventurer."

Pasha's eyes shot wide open. "Oh, now Kadmik makes for a good display!"

"Hush, now, Pash," Winimar said, giving his tone a rough edge. "I'm talking to the detective."

Pasha went silent and sulked.

Winimar said, "Anyway, I shouted out and imagine my surprise when the shadow answered back!"

"What did it say?" I said.

"Well, that's the thing. I dunno. Fell asleep, I figure, right there and then. Next thing I know, I wake up in this here bed with my Pasha at my side." He took his wife's hand, and they smiled at each other.

"Do you recall what the shadow said, at all?"

He shook his head. "Nothing. Only I know it spoke. Deep voice. But I don't remember the words. Or even if it was words." He shrugged. "That is all there was to it. Glad the shadow, or whoever it was didn't have a mind to do anything to me while I slept the night away on that floor."

Pasha made a tsk-tsk sound, and held his hand closer.

I said, "So you are aware items were taken that night?"

Pasha said, "I just told him after he woke up not two hours ago. As big a surprise to him as one would expect."

"Yeah, I'm aware now," he said. "Disappointed that I had to be the one on duty. Now I get all the blame."

"No one is blaming you for anything, Mister Hubertus. I'm just trying to get the facts as you remember them."

"Oh, he got the blame, all right," Pasha said. "That blow hard Othmar said as much when he was here."

"He came here?"

Pasha scowled. "Yeah, and not in a good manner of way, either. Hollered and yelled so much the nurses had to get an orderly to ask him to leave." She looked at Hubertus. "Blamed him for all of it. Said he must have been in on the job. Or if not, was foolish enough to let it happen. Like Hub here could defend himself from being spelled. Can you believe it?"

"He fired me," Hubertus said. "Told poor Pash, here, that once I woke up she was to inform me that my employment was terminated."

I said, "I don't think Mister Othmar has the legal grounds to do that."

"Legal or not, I'm fired now," he said, looking mournful. "My cousin had to pull all sorts of strings to get me that job, and now I'm back looking for work."

"And with a hospital bill to pay for now, too!" Pasha said.

Winimar patted her hand. "We'll check out, today, sweetheart. Don't you worry."

I asked him, "Do you recall anything unusual that night, before you were spelled, while making your rounds? Anything at all."

"Nothing, ma'am. Was the same as any other night."

There was nothing else to ask at that moment although I intended to follow up with him once more facts from the case came to light.

"We will leave you for now, Mr. Hubertus," I said. "Perhaps later we can talk once you are feeling better. Which reminds me. Might I get your address?"

"Yes, all right," he said, and I wrote it down.

I thanked them both and turned to leave when I realized something. To Pasha, I asked, "Mrs. Hubertus, what did the other detective ask you while he was here?"

She blinked at me as if trying to remember. "Oh, not much, really. Since Win was fast asleep as a newborn babe, there wasn't much he could ask. Oh, I remember. He wanted to know if me or Win here knew of a woman."

"What woman?" I said.

She scrunched her face up with thought. "Ip-Horn, I think."

I recalled the name on the back of the bookstore business card. "Ipthorn, perhaps?"

Pasha's face brightened. "That's what it was. Ipthorn. Strange name that."

"Did he ask anything else? Maybe why he was enquiring about this Ipthorn woman?"

Pasha shook her head. "No," she said with a shrug. "And we know no one by that name."

Thanking them for their time, Fairfax and I withdrew to the hallway.

"Let's talk to the Warding Master," I said to Fairfax before he could speak. I knew what he would say.

After searching the halls, I spotted her. Unlike the nurses and doctors who wore white, the Warding Master wore a deep red robe with black swirling patterns.

I approached her and introduced myself.

She smiled and said, "I am Master Dorchen. How can I help?"

"Were you the one who removed the spell on Mr. Hubertus?"

"Yes, I did. Bit of work that one."

"How so?"

"Well, the sleep spell that was cast had been enhanced. Perhaps with a minor artifact, or a detailed charm."

"Is such a spell common?"

Master Dorchen frowned with thought. "Yes, and no. The sleep spell can be cast on its own with a moderate level of skill. But what was done to him could have been fatal if the caster was so inclined. With just an extra word, he could have been put to sleep forever."

"Do you know of anyone with that level of skill?"

Master Dorchen chuckled. "There are dozens of mid-level practitioners in the area with the ability, and an equal number of greater ones. I could do it easily enough. But that would be unethical by the laws that govern spell casters."

I realized that magic weaving and casting was more or less common, but I hoped for a short list of suspects.

"Might I ask you another question. This one may seem... strange."

The Warding Master smiled. "Strange is my business."

"Have you ever heard of someone turned to stone before?"

Dorchen's smile vanished. "Turned to stone? Are you serious?"

She saw I was.

"Well," she said. "There are no spells in existence which can do such a terrible thing. Perhaps something from the Pre-Era, in the dark times. But nothing now. That is for certain."

I made a mental note to quiz this woman again, once the Chief Constable gave his permission to reveal how Oswall died. Instead, I thanked her, and she nodded and went about her rounds.

Fairfax and I trundled down the stairs and stood outside the main entrance. It felt good to breathe fresh air again.

Sensing Fairfax wanted to speak I said, "Go ahead, say your peace, Constable."

Fairfax said, "I hate to kick up the point but I believe this clearly makes it."

"And that would be?"

"That whoever is responsible for this burglary is most likely not the same person who killed Oswall. It does not add up. Why put this man to sleep when he could have just as easily turned him to stone?"

It was a good point I had to admit and sighed. "I will concede that it may well be two different individuals. But I am not ready to give up on this angle and search through all those other files for another. We've pulled on this thread, so let us follow through with it."

Fairfax nodded. "Very well. What did you have in mind now?"

"What time is it?"

He pulled out his pocket watch. "Coming up on one o'clock."

"There is still time before Curator Othmar's airship arrives." I held up the business card. "I want to learn more about Oswall's interest in this Ipthorn woman. So, Constable, let us go shopping for books."

CHAPTER SEVEN

The quaint storefront of Rousset's Tomes & Books of Rarity was on a busy street off Stage Court, nestled between a clockworks toy store and a custom rock light shop.

Fairfax opened the store's door for me and a bell overhead rang as we entered.

I took in the sight of so many books. Every available spot was packed with them. They lined every shelf, and the shelves went as high as the ceiling. Tall stacks of books towered up from the floor and wedged against each other. Others were secured within cabinets of thick glass. Everywhere, books. And it smelled as a bookstore should, like old parchment.

A little man was snoozing in a large comfy chair in one corner. He had a tea cup in one hand. Surprised that the door bell did not wake him Fairfax cleared his throat.

At this horrid noise the man's eyes flew open. "Oh, hello!" The man said with a cheerful tone. He put his cup down on the table and stood while rubbing the sleep from his eyes.

"How might I help you?" He asked as he approached. He was smartly dressed in a white-collared shirt and tie, dark trousers, and an apron covered in inky smudges. Upon his nose perched a slender pair of glasses. To me, he looked more like a banker than a bookseller. "Would you like some tea, perhaps?" he said motioning to a table with a teakettle and cups. "I just made it fresh. Can never get enough of it."

I politely declined the tea, then introduced ourselves and asked, "Might you be the owner of this fine establishment?"

The little man beamed at the compliment. "Why, yes I am. My name is Misael Rousset. A pleasure to meet you both." He gave Fairfax's uniform a curious look. "Is everything all right?"

"I hope so," I said. "We have a few questions if you can spare a moment."

Misael laughed and waved a hand around him. "As you can see, I am not fighting off any customers. In fact, customers are a little scarce, nowadays. People regard books as more of a luxury than a necessity, I'm afraid."

I considered that statement a crime all on its own. "Did a Detective Oswall visit you in the last few days, by chance?"

He pursed his lips in thought, then said, "Why, I believe a detective came by here a short while ago. But I missed him as I was picking up a new lot of books I won at auction that day. He spoke to my assistant though."

"Is your assistant here?"

"Oh, I'm afraid not. She called in sick yesterday morning, poor thing."

"And what is her name?"

"Elicia. Elicia Ipthorn," Misael said.

"Did she mention what the detective said while he was here?"

At this question, Misael's amiability faltered. He gave us a worried look. "Why? Is everything okay? Did something happen?"

I gave him my most reassuring smile. "We wish to speak with Miss Ipthorn, is all. Might you have her address?"

"Ah, yes. Yes, of course. Let me get it for you," he said, and hurried over to a counter and flipped through a note book.

I gave the shop another look. Why did Oswall come here? To speak with Ipthorn specifically or another reason? The owner, maybe? "Mr. Rousset, I am astounded by the sheer number of books you've amassed. How long have you run this shop?"

Misael wrote on a piece of paper as he answered. "Oh, well, quite a while. Thirty-eight years, I believe. And I have more books than this. My house is filled with the overflow, plus a storage warehouse crammed full."

He walked over and handed me the piece of paper with an address in the Hearts district. "I think she still lives there or at least she didn't mentioned if she'd moved again."

"Does she move a lot?" Fairfax asked.

"Ah, well, these are hard times. And as you can see, the customers are fewer and fewer each year. So I can't pay very much. I know Elicia has been struggling as of late, so I allow her to leave early on occasion to find part time work in the evening. As a result, I fear she has had to move around a little, finding a place she can afford."

Misael looked saddened by Elicia's predicament.

I nodded in commiseration.

Fairfax said, "You have such a large stock, sir. But do you also specialize in any particular kind of book as well?"

The question made me wonder what the constable was going on about.

Misael's face lit up. "Yes! My one great fondness is for old books which recount the histories. Especially tomes that originate from those eras. They make for marvellous reading. The tales they tell far outmatch what modern fictional authors can muster, in my opinion."

"I notice you have a section on iconography right over there," Fairfax said.

"Oh, yes," Misael said. "I've made it a point to read as many as I can. And I do have a lot of time on my hands." He laughed.

Fairfax gave me a knowing little smile.

It was as if he'd hit me over the head. "Mr. Rousset," I said. "Might you be keen on looking at something for us?"

"Certainly."

I pulled out the etching and spread the paper on a stack of books.

Misael adjusted his glasses and peered at it. "My, my," he said with appreciation. "This is quite a symbol you have here. Might I ask where you got it?"

I glanced at Fairfax, who shrugged. I said, "We've been finding this mark engraved at various places around town."

"Hand engraved, do you know, or magically done?" Misael asked.

"I found this one magically created," I said. "Why? Does it make a difference?"

"Yes, actually. It might give you an indication whether the individual who left it is a worshipper."

"Worshipper?"

"Yes," Misael said. He blinked at our curious looks and explained. "This isn't just an engraving. It is a religious symbol. A very old one as well. If it was magically produced, I would guess it was ceremonial in function."

I did not like the sound of that. "Do you know what this symbol represents?"

"Oh, I forget how to pronounce the name. Just a moment," he said and went over to the shelves of iconography books. "Here we are," he said, removing one. He carried it over, placed it down and thumbed through the old pages. I could see images within, each strange and archaic.

Misael spoke as he searched. "This looks like the Mark of an Ancient One. Well before the Pre-Era. So old that little is known of the Gods which reigned then. Myths are our only source of their existence. Ah, here we are." He turned the book around so we could see.

On the page was a drawing of a squid the size of an elephant, its tentacles wrapped around a warrior figure, devouring him.

"It doesn't look very big," I noted. Most drawings of the godlike beings of that time frame were colossal, stomping on cities and such. For Ancient Gods, this one was quite puny.

"Well, with regards to size, it doesn't matter when you are God. I would not want to mess with any of them."

"Does it have a name?" I asked.

Misael read off the page. "Quantiqtl," he said, and laughed. "Try saying that while in your cups."

"You think this etching could be a Mark of this Quantiqtl?"

He turned to the next page, and pointed. "See for yourself."

This page contained a different drawing. It, too, was of a squid but much more rudimentary. In fact, it looked almost identical to the etching on the paper.

Misael said, "This sort of iconography is typical. Worshippers needed to draw the symbol that best represented their god. Not everyone is an artist, so this style served that purpose and its easier when magically produced."

He pointed at the etching on the paper. "I'd guess this was most likely done by someone who worships Quantiqtl and maybe as part of a ceremony."

Fairfax asked, "Are there still worshippers of the Old Gods?"

"Across all of human history there have been thousands of deities in the pantheon of Gods. Some fade, yes. But there will always be a small group, or cult, that keeps the spirit of a God alive. So, yes, most certainly people still actively worship them."

As Fairfax and I took our leave there were new worrying questions on my mind.

Were we dealing with cultists and, if so, why did they murder Oswall?

CHAPTER EIGHT

We returned to High Garden Museum, and when I rang the bell this time there was an answer.

One of the huge doors swung open and a tall gaunt man with round spectacles peered out.

"Yes, what is it now?" the man said. Upon seeing Fairfax's uniform the man brightened. "Did you find the stolen relics so soon? That's wonderful!"

I shook my head. "No, we haven't found them, yet. Are you Curator Aubert Othmar?"

The man's expression collapsed to one of disappointment. "Well, I guess solving this simple crime was expecting too much of the Constabulary."

I was taken aback, but did not want to get into an argument. "Sir, we need to view the scene of the burglary and ask you a few questions."

The man, obviously Aubert, sputtered a laugh. "Are you joking? Again? Are there two Constabularies in town conducting separate investigations and I was not made aware of that fact? Am I expected to repeat everything over again? Nonsense!"

I felt Fairfax tense up beside me.

Aubert looked angry, "Where is Detective Oswall? Knocked off for a drink at the pub already, hmm? The man was practically soaked in whiskey when he bumbled about the place. Well? Where is this drunk?"

Fairfax leaned in, and said, "Detective Oswall was murdered this morning."

Aubert Othmar stared at us in stunned silence. He blinked and looked from Fairfax to me. "Is... is this true?"

"Unfortunately, yes," I said. "We are here to resume his investigation into your case." And see if it had something to do with his death. I did not say that out loud.

The curator shook his head, regaining his composure. "Why, yes, of course. Please come inside." He backed out of the way and Fairfax and I entered.

The main foyer was gigantic with a high vaulted ceilings and glossy marble floors. The walls were lined with a diorama of all the great wars which stretched deeper into the building. Smaller displays filled the space in between with weapons, pottery and bits of armor.

"Sorry to hear about the detective," Aubert said as he shut the great door with a loud clang. He seemed to mean it despite his initial tirade.

I introduced ourselves, then asked, "Are there any employees here now?"

Aubert shook his head. "No, but we will be open tomorrow on schedule. I didn't want any unsupervised activities here while I was away."

"You were in the Capital?"

"Yes. My superiors at the Capital Museum wanted answers regarding the theft of the relics. But I was unable to offer them anything since I had not spoken to Detective Oswall for a few days." He frowned when mentioning the detective.

Fairfax asked, "And where were you the night of the burglary?"

"I was at home with my wife. We were entertaining friends from the coast who are staying with us. I was there all night. You can check with them if it pleases you."

Fairfax nodded.

"Might we look at the vault?" I asked.

"Of course," Aubert said, nodding. "It's down in the basement sub-level."

We followed the curator toward a side doorway, passing detailed displays of beautiful paintings and other art work. At the door, Aubert produced a key ring and unlocked it.

At the sight of the key ring, I asked, "Did Hubertus have keys to the vault room, too?"

Aubert frowned. "Yes, and that is a mistake I will not be making with the next night caretaker, I can tell you that." He glared at me. "I think your investigation will be shortened if you looked into that man. That is the last time I hire someone as a favor. He had access to everything!"

"He told us you fired him," I said.

"What? You spoke to him? He's awake now?"

"Yes. We saw him earlier today. And he's doing fine," I said, knowing Aubert wouldn't be concerned.

"The incompetence of that fellow. This place is very secure and yet he managed to let someone break in."

Fairfax said, "He was spelled. Hard to protect against that."

"Regardless," Aubert said. "Spelled or not who is to say he wasn't in on it from the beginning? Let the person in and allow himself to be put to sleep to make him look like a victim."

"We are considering every angle, Mr. Othmar. That is one of them."

This mollified the curator, and he led us through the door and descended a series of stairs. We then passed through another series of locked doors until arriving in a small room crammed with carvings, art and armor. In one corner sat a large free-standing vault safe.

"Here it is," Aubert said and went over to it. "Do you want to see inside?"

"Please."

He worked the combination dial while mumbling to himself. I found myself looking for engravings of squids on the walls but found none.

The vault door clanked and Aubert pulled it open with a grunt. The inside was jammed with a variety of objects. Conspicuously, there was a narrow barren spot on one of its shelves.

"The trunk was located there?" I asked.

"Yes," Aubert said. "A recent delivery from the Capital Museum. We received it only a week prior, and now it's gone. Strange, really."

"Why do you say that?"

Aubert waved his hand. "There are countless other items here for the taking, many of them extremely valuable, even priceless from a historical perspective. Yet, this trunk was the only thing they bothered with."

Fairfax asked, "Who has access to this room?"

"Well, that would only be myself and the night caretaker. There is another set of keys back in the Capital Museum for insurance purposes, and they still have it, I checked."

"So the caretaker's keys are gone now?" I asked.

"Yes, unfortunately. I have a locksmith coming from the Capital to replace everything. After this nonsense I cannot trust a local one to do it."

"And who else has the combination for the vault?"

"Just myself here, and it's recorded back at the Capital."

"Is there any way someone might have obtained the vault combination from you?"

Aubert looked indignant. "Of course not. I have it memorized only. Other than at the Capital Museum there is no other written record of it."

I looked at the vault closer. It was an older model, but sturdy. From what I could see it had not been forced open. Physically, anyways.

"It might be possible that magic had been invoked to open it," I said.

"I considered that," said Aubert. "It is always a risk when trying to keep these items secure. Mundane methods are too basic a security measure when magic is a factor. Almost impossible. I'm at a point where I must hire a full time Warding Master to live on the premises to keep spell-casting burglars away." He looked forlorn.

I took the case folder out of my satchel and opened it to the trunk's item list. "Do you know off hand the value of these items?"

Aubert shrugged. "That is subjective. For collectors, historians and museums they have a value, but from a historical perspective. For the average layman they are just old trinkets."

"Do they have magical properties?"

"Some do, to varying degrees but that point is moot."

"How so?"

"Well, they are soul-bound relics. Meaning no one else other than their original owners can use them. And the owners of these items have been dead for centuries. Millennia, even. So, as far as magical worth, they have none. Mere curiosities than anything."

I knew first hand that this statement was not entirely true. "Yes, but couldn't a descendant use them? There have been instances of relics passed down for generations."

Aubert waved a dismissive hand. "To a limited extent that is correct. A direct descendant might bring forth the magical element of the item. But unless you knew first hand who that descendant was, it would be almost impossible to find out. And even then, the item may do nothing at all. Which is why they are relegated to mere curiosities."

"Why is that?"

The curator raised his hands at the items around us. "These are so old and the cataloguing of them so poor that finding even the original owner's identity is difficult. So how is it possible to track the descendants of a person when that person is unknown to begin with?"

I looked at the list. "The names of these items denote their magical properties?"

"Yes, as far as research can figure out. No one can know what their true properties are anymore. We use historical records to learn more about them. Many may not even be what they are listed as because so little information is available. So, to answer your original question, they are, for all intents and purposes, worthless."

"So why would someone steal them and leave these valuable items alone?"

Aubert shrugged. "That is your job to find out, detective."

True, I thought. Then I looked at the trunk's item list again. One stood out.

"Curator Othmar, I see a 'Gunther's Kaggik Talon?' listed."

"Yes, so?"

"What does Kaggik mean?" I had my suspicions.

"Well, Kaggik derives from the ancient language of Sennia. Its general meaning is rock or stone."

"Gunther's Stone Talon," I said, with a sense of dread growing in my gut. "And what did this Stone Talon do?"

"Well, detective, according to myth," Aubert said, "it turned people to stone."

I looked to Fairfax who arched a brow. Then to Aubert, I asked, "Turned people to stone? Are you certain?"

Aubert nodded. "It is one of the few myths for which we have multiple sources. Gunther the Ungrateful had created it from the talon of a gorgon. Then he ran around turning the legions of the Gods to stone. Even turned some of the Ancient Ones to stone, too, if that is to be believed."

Fairfax asked, "But only Gunther's descendants can use the magic in the talon, correct?"

"Well, yes, but the talon can never be used ever again. It's inert as the others."

"But Gunther's descendants -", Fairfax said, but Aubert held up a hand.

"Gunther was a eunuch from a very young age. It was a necessary requirement to create magical artifacts. So, no. No descendants of

Gunther's could ever exist. And, as a result, the Talon has never been used since his death, thousands of years ago."

Until this morning, I wanted to say but didn't. With this revelation I needed time to think.

We took our leave and told the curator we'd return later. He did not look convinced, but said nothing more as he closed the Museum's front door behind us.

For a few moments, Fairfax and I just stood on the top step, taking in the view below of the gardens.

"Gunther's Stone Talon," Fairfax said. "You were right and that cat was right. This case is directly connected to Oswall's death."

"But how can the Talon be used now after all this time?" I said.

"Perhaps the myths were wrong. The ones regarding Gunther being a eunuch. Or he's been resurrected by some arcane means?"

I sighed. "Well, we now know what the potential murder weapon is. And regardless of whether the person using it has anything to do with Gunther, the fact remains they are out there now and they might use it again."

Fairfax asked, "So where to next?"

"I'm curious as to why Oswall had an interest in Elicia Ipthorn," I said.

"Maybe he took a liking to her. Wanted to court her," Fairfax said with a wry grin.

I grinned back. "Then let us go ask her."

CHAPTER NINE

The Hearts District, one of the poorest areas of town, was filled with dilapidated buildings which stood as a testament to its poverty.

The address Rousset had given took us to its eastern most edge. Any more further and we'd end up in the town dump.

Fairfax parked the buggy in front of the end unit of a cramped row of townhouses. All the curtains were drawn, and windows closed. It may have been my suspicious mind, but that seemed unusual on such a warm day.

"Maybe she's out?" Fairfax said.

"Only one way to be sure, Constable," I said and got out of the buggy.

A large woman leaned out of a window of the townhouse next to Elicia's. Her long blonde hair wrapped in a bun and with arms like giant hams, pink and sweaty as she stirred a huge bowl of dough.

As we climbed the stairs to the little alcove, which protected the front door from rain, Fairfax tipped his cap to the large woman. "Good afternoon," he said.

"Afternoon," she said and watched us intently.

I exchanged a glance with Fairfax who kept his expression neutral. Once we had stepped into the alcove Fairfax knocked on the door. After several minutes, he did so again. I tried peering through the nearest window but the curtains blocked my view.

Still no answer. Fairfax tried the doorknob, but found it locked.

"We should try back later," I suggested and Fairfax nodded.

As we descended the stairs the large woman in the window said, "Looking for Elicia?"

"Yes, do you know if she is home?" I said.

"I don't think so," she said. Her stirring never stopped. "Might want to try at her work. It's a bookstore."

"We did. The owner said Elicia had sent word yesterday morning she had taken ill."

"Oh, well then, she probably went to be with her sister up in Creekside. She's always going there."

"When was the last time you saw him?"

The woman screwed her face up. "About two days ago. Didn't look sick to me but what do I know? I'm no doctor."

I thanked her, and we returned to stand next to the buggy. To Fairfax, I said, "I'd like to get a peek inside."

Fairfax shrugged. "Afraid kicking the door in might upset the neighbor, and she'd chase us around with a rolling pin. Besides, we can't go in without justification. Calling in sick doesn't cover that, I'm afraid."

"You're no fun, Fairfax," I teased. I had a hunch and glanced in my satchel. The clasp was brass.

"Well, now. It appears something is amiss."

"One of them wants to pop out?" Fairfax said. He looked a little eager.

I glanced up at the building. The woman had gone from her window. "Let's try the door again," I said and climbed back up the stairs before Fairfax could protest.

Under the alcove, I placed the satchel on the welcome mat at the door. I opened it wide and touched the clasp. The knitting bag wiggled around and a cat's head popped up from it. This one was a light brown color. Its eyes the same as the others, a rainbow spectrum.

I asked the cat, "Where is Elicia Ipthorn?"

It jumped from the bag and landed on the floor. It stared at the door a moment then placed a single paw on it. I heard the lock come undone. The knob turned, and the door eased open a few inches. The brown cat then leapt into the bag and was gone.

Fairfax looked alarmed. "I believe we just committed breaking and entering."

I shook my head, "Something is not right. She wouldn't have opened the door, otherwise."

Fairfax nodded once and withdrew his pistol. He stepped up to the door as I took up the satchel again and reached in to put a hand on my pistol.

Fairfax knocked and shouted with a loud, commanding voice. "Police! Is anyone here? Please announce your presence!"

No one answered, and Fairfax pushed the door wider. There was a short hallway and a set of stairs leading to the second level with a sitting room to the right. The place was quiet.

As we entered Fairfax motioned for me to stay. It was standard procedure, but it still bothered me. I wanted to be the one going in first.

As I watched the stairs Fairfax moved down the hall, pistol at the ready. At the end on the right was another room and Fairfax stepped before the doorway. Then he gasped.

"What? What is it?" I said, my body tensing.

Fairfax stepped out of sight and returned a moment later. He hurried through the hall. "Another one."

"Statue?" I asked.

He nodded. "Let me check the upstairs first."

I tried to not let my frustration show as I waited for Fairfax to sweep the second floor. When he appeared on the stairs again he said, "Nothing up there. Better go take a look."

I walked to the end of the hall, my heart thumping in my chest.

It was a kitchen, and engraved on one of its walls was the Mark of Quantiqtl. Sitting on a chair at the kitchen table, teacup to her mouth, was a woman completely made of stone.

xxx

56

As Fairfax went to use the closest police call-box, I searched the house. The downstairs turned up nothing. No signs of struggle or forced entry, and the back door was locked. Since the front door had been locked as well, I could only assume the perpetrator had used Elicia's own keys when he left. The kitchen table had been set for tea with one cup, now stone, at Elicia's pursed lips ready to sip it. The other teacup was empty.

I checked the upstairs. Only a simple bedroom and water closet. But in the bedroom, spread out on the bed, were a pair of open suitcases full of clothes and sundries. I checked the drawers and closet and found little of note. It appeared that everything Elicia held dear were in these suitcases.

Then I noticed a small glass bottle wedged between the clothing in one of them. I recognized the medical symbols on its hand written label. 'Dream Berries of Ogden'. Perhaps she had trouble sleeping?

Fairfax rejoined me at the front door. "Boys are coming now. Did you check out the back?"

Starting from the back door we searched the yard. The cobblestone ground showed no footprints. A line of Elicia's laundry blew in the wind. She would never take them down now.

I wanted to speak with the neighbor again so leaving Fairfax to watch the townhouse, I went next door. After an initial shock and fluttering of hands the neighbor woman, named Farrah, let me in and sat me on a tiny couch. She sat across from me, tears flowing down her cheeks.

"You are sure she is dead?" Farrah asked, eyes wide in bewilderment.

"I'm afraid so," I said. I gave her a few more moments, and asked. "You said you saw her a couple days ago? Could you be more specific?"

Farrah sniffled and snorted into a handkerchief. "Yes. It must have been two evenings past that I saw her coming back from the store with a bag of groceries. We exchanged pleasantries, and she went in."

I considered the packed suitcases on Elicia's bed. "Do you know if Elicia was planning a trip? Or intended to go somewhere for a visit?"

This question befuddled Farrah even more, but just when I worried she was going to breakdown again, she said, "Well, she told me she was going to sell a book."

"A book?"

"Yeah. Not sure what she was going on about. Kind of a simple girl, homely like. But she was positive she could get a lot of money for it and she'd leave for the South Islands and never return."

"Did she mention to whom she was going to sell it?"

Farrah shook her head and cried again.

I told her a constable would be by to take a formal statement and I went back to Elicia's townhouse. The constables had arrived by then and Fairfax sent most out to canvass the neighborhood.

As I entered the kitchen with Fairfax, I found Constable Webster looking at Elicia sitting in her stone chair. He scratched at the hair under his cap and said, "Now how are we going to move this one?"

To Fairfax, I said, "Look at the teacup. It's empty and unstained. I believe Elicia was waiting for someone to arrive and was drinking. Then she let the person in, probably through the back door and they both sat down here. All this indicates she was familiar with that person."

"But who?" Fairfax said.

"A buyer for a book she was selling," I said. "And she thought she'd be paid handsomely for it. The bags upstairs show she was ready to leave after the sale. The buyer, once he received his book, then turned her to stone and left that Mark. He exited out the back and used her keys to lock it behind him."

"But what book?" Fairfax said.

"That is what I intend to find out. Come Fairfax, we must go talk to Misael Rousset, again, at once."

CHAPTER TEN

Misael Rousset was closing the store for the day when we pulled up out front. He stood in the open doorway and looked at us with worry.

"Oh, dear," Misael said as we exited the buggy. "I take it things are not well and fine?"

"Unfortunately, no," I said. "I'm sorry to inform you that Miss Ipthorn is dead."

Misael gasped in shock and clutched at his chest. "By the Gods! No!"

Fairfax and I shuffled him into the store and made him sit before he dropped of a heart attack. Misael slumped in the chair, a look of horror on his face. "Oh, that sweet girl. This is terrible. How did it happen? Do you know who did it?"

I shook my head. "We are working on the who, but as to the how, I was hoping maybe your knowledge of the histories may be of assistance."

Regaining his composure, Misael straightened in his chair and wiped a handkerchief over his face. "Yes. Yes, of course. How may I help?"

I looked at Fairfax who shrugged. I then explained to Misael how both Elicia and Oswall had been turned to stone. With further explanation about what Curator Othmar had told us of Gunther's Stone Talon Misael's expression morphed to one of sheer amazement.

"Gunther's Stone Talon? Been used again? Impossible!"

"And yet there are two victims of its power and we fear there may be more," I said.

"But there's no way for the Talon to be used other than by Gunther the Ungrateful who is thankfully long dead. And everyone knows he lacked the... er... ability to father children."

I nodded. "True enough but there might be something which may account for the Talon's reuse."

"And that is?"

"Elicia was trying to sell a book. A very expensive book which may contain the missing link."

"Which book is that?" Misael asked.

"I was hoping you might be able tell use, Mr. Rousset. I believe Elicia stole it from your store with the intent to sell it to her killer."

Misael gaped like a landed fish as he tried to absorb this revelation. "No! Not Elicia. She wouldn't do anything like that to me. Not after all I've done for her."

"That may be so, but she was having a difficult time financially, as you already told us. It would not be too much of a stretch to allow that she may have decided that selling one of your books would save her from that difficulty."

Now Misael looked confused, still not willing to accept what Elicia had done.

Fairfax asked, "Are you missing any books?"

Misael blinked at the question. "I don't know. Well, not that I would have noticed. There are quite a bit here." He looked around at his store and the tens of thousands of volumes. "I'd have to do an inventory. Even my expensive ones number in the thousands." He motioned to the dozens of large enclosed cabinets. "It would take days, weeks even to go through them and check against my inventory list."

Fairfax said, "I can get the boys to come in, start to sift through this lot with Mr. Rousset's list."

For the first time in my life I regretted the sight of so many wonderful books in one place. The undertaking would be horrendous and in the meantime there could be other victims of the Stone Talon.

Hopeful for some guidance I looked at the knitting bag. To my grand relief the clasp was brass.

Fairfax noticed my expression. "What? They want to come out again so soon? Is that a record for one day?"

"No, not a record, thankfully." I put the satchel on the ground.

Misael looked at our exchange, befuddled. "Might I ask what you two are going on about?"

Fairfax smiled at him, "Stand back, Mr. Rousset, and you will see for yourself."

I exposed the knitting bag and touched the clasp. It yawned open and began to wiggle.

"Oh, my dear!" Misael said and recoiled in the chair.

A cat's head appeared. This one was orange with white spots.

I asked the cat, "What book did Elicia Ipthorn steal?"

The cat did not move. It only watched me with an intent stare.

Fairfax asked Misael, "Sir, if we knew which cabinet the book was stored in would that help you narrow the search?"

Misael was staring wide eye at the cat, but turned to answer Fairfax. "Well, yes, it would. But what can a cat do to help? Strange place to keep a cat if you ask me. Cruel even."

Fairfax chuckled.

This time, I asked the cat, "From which cabinet did Elicia Ipthorn steal a book?"

The cat launched itself from the bag startling Misael who yelped in fright. The orange cat trotted over to one of the smaller heavy oak cabinets.

"Your cat is well trained, Detective, but I don't see how it will -", he stopped talking as he watched.

The cat lifted one paw and touched the cabinet door. There was an audible click as the lock came undone, then the door swung open on its own.

"By the Gods!" Misael proclaimed in astonishment.

Inside the cabinet were rows of drawers. The cat moved closer and stared up at a drawer near the top. That drawer also clicked and slid open. Then the cat scampered back to the satchel and vanished into the bag with a jump.

Misael stared in utter disbelief. His eyes went from the bag to me, then to the bag again. "That's... that's the Bag of Infinite Cats." He regarded me, awestruck. "That means you're the direct descendant of -", he said before I interrupted.

"Who I am descended from means nothing at this moment as there is a murderer running around the town."

Misael still stared at me in amazement.

Frustrated, I said, "Please, Mr. Rousset, if you will?" I motioned to the cabinet.

The bookshop keeper snapped out of his trance. "Yes. Yes, of course. Let's take a look." He walked to the cabinet, but gave me a frightened glance.

He would be happy to pay me a gold piece for that little show, I thought with mild amusement.

Misael looked into the open cabinet. "Empty," he said, his brow furrowing. He removed a clipboard from the cabinet's inner paneling and ran a finger down a list. He stopped, with a look of confusion. "Well, that is peculiar."

"What is?" I asked.

"There is a missing book, but not one of any real value. The title roughly translates to Magical Sources and Rebirths. Mad Scribe Perrick Faywin was the author. It is almost complete gibberish, something even the most ardent translator would be unable to decipher beyond bits and pieces of text."

"Magical Sources and Rebirths," I said. "Do you have any idea what it contained?" And why someone would kill for it?

"Yes, well, not much is known about it. From the fragments of sentences which could be understood, Perrick had a fascination with breaking magic down to its most basic essence. He believed any spell or item could have its magical elements reversed. But nothing of the sort can be done, or has been done. Not even at the Citadel. It's an impossibility."

I let this information sink into my tired old brain for a moment. "Might such a theory result in an artifact having its soul-bound limitation broken? So it could be bound to someone else?"

Misael eyebrows beetled on his forehead. "Well, perhaps. But we are dealing with the fanciful ravings of a lunatic. Perrick was not known for being sane. He was called the Mad Scribe, after all."

My thoughts raced with the potential implications of this.

When Fairfax noticed my distraction, he asked Misael, "How long was this book in your possession?"

"Oh, a little over a week. Picked it up as part of a lot sale at the auction house."

"Did anyone bid against you?"

"No one. But that is typical. There is little interest in books as an investment now a days."

Until now, I thought. "Did anyone come to your store and ask for the book?"

Misael's face froze. "Oh, by the Gods. Yes! A man came in about four days ago and asked for the tome by name. He was a strange one, too."

"Can you describe him?" Fairfax asked.

"He was tall and skinny. Wore all black clothing. Funny looking nose, too. Long and hook shaped. But that wasn't what was strange about him."

Tired of waiting for a straight answer, I asked, "What was strange?"

"Well, he wore make-up."

"Make-up?" Fairfax said.

"Yes, white make-up all over his face. He looked to be a mime on a shopping trip. It made me assume he had a condition of the skin which needed the outrageous application."

"And he offered to buy the book?" I asked.

"Yes, but I refused to sell it to him."

"Why is that?"

"After only spending a few moments with the man, I realized I just didn't like him. And when I refused, he raised his price. Double, then triple! Still, even though the money would have been useful, his desperation to obtain the book put me off. I told him it was not for sale and asked him to leave."

"Did you get a name?"

"Unfortunately, no. Though by his demeanor, I suspect it would have been as fake as his face."

"What happened when you asked him to leave?"

"Well, he ranted and raved, calling me unprofessional and then left. I pushed out the entire incident from my mind." He looked at the empty drawer with realization dawning on his face. "And now I see that by my refusing to sell him that book has resulted in Elicia losing her life. The poor woman."

I did not argue the last point. "Was Elicia here during this exchange?"

"Yes, she was."

"Then I think either he approached her about purchasing the tome, or she contacted him somehow."

Misael shook his head. "I'd suspect the former. Poor Elicia wasn't the brightest girl. The notion to steal from me was beyond her realm of capability. She had to have been coerced."

"That is a possibility," I said, though mostly to make the man feel a little better.

"But how did Elicia get the book from the cabinet? The keys are always on my person."

"I believe your love of tea was how she did it."

"What do you mean?" Misael asked.

"I found a bottle of sleep berries at her townhouse. It would not have been a stretch for her to drop one in your tea and wait until you fell asleep to take the keys from you. Then after she stole the book, and secreted it away, she returned them."

Misael went silent, hurt by the betrayal of one he trusted.

As Fairfax and I were leaving Misael said, "Please. As a favor to me and poor Elicia, find this man and make him pay for what he has done." There was anger in this gentle man's eyes.

"Of that, Mr. Rousset," I said, "I promise."

CHAPTER ELEVEN

We left the bookshop keeper with his regrets and returned to the buggy.

"So we need to find a tall, rude, skinny man covered in all black attire and wearing women's make-up," Fairfax said. "Should not take us long."

"I admit our list of suspects is still as non-existent as when we started. But this revelation about the book Elicia stole provides a few answers," I said.

"How so?"

"The suspect stole the Talon from the museum, but could not use it. It was inert. So the suspect tries to get the Magic Sources & Rebirth book from Rousset. Maybe he did not know of its existence until after the auction. When he could not purchase the book, he manipulated Elicia into stealing it."

Fairfax nodded. "He meets her at her home, going through the back door at night. Then he... turns her to stone?"

I held up a finger. "Not yet. The Talon is still useless at that point. So he checks the book to confirm its validity, finds the spell within its pages and reads it somehow. He must be versed in the language. The spell works, breaks the soul-binding on the Talon from Gunther the Ungrateful, and binds it to himself."

"How do you bind an artifact?"

"By touch," I said, and did not want to get into the details for which I was familiar. "So once the artifact is bound to him, his first act is to test the Talon on poor Elicia."

"As she was drinking her tea, daydreaming of her future life in the South Islands."

"Yes, but why he would desire the Talon, specifically, is beyond me. If he wanted to kill someone using a pistol would work just as well."

"But less grand a spectacle."

I shrugged, "As to his true motivations for trying to obtain the Talon and get it bound to himself, I am at a loss."

Fairfax said, "So why kill Oswall?"

"He must have found a connection to the suspect, or was getting too close for comfort. Then he was lured to Muddy Way on some pretext and turned to stone."

"Oswall knew of Elicia. Wrote her name on that card for a reason. How did he make the connection between the museum burglary and Elicia? There must be an overlap."

I pondered that. "He was pulling on a thread we missed." Then I sighed. "Ah, Fairfax we've gotten ourselves tangled up in some ugly business. It makes me tired."

"Let's report in at the Constabulary, then I will take you home. We will pick up first thing in the morning. And I will bring biscuits this time."

That made me laugh, which was what I needed.

We drove back to the Constabulary as the sun was setting on the horizon. As we turned into the lot there was a large open backed truck parked there. A small crane atop it was lowering something wrapped in canvas to the ground. Constable Webster was supervising, shouting instructions to two men working the crane.

He nodded to us as we approached. "Finally managed to get him here in one piece. Took a bit of work, too."

I must have been more tired than I realized because it then hit me that the object being lowered was Detective Oswall.

"Well done, Constable," I said.

Fairfax looked around the lot. "Where are you going to... uh... store him?"

"He's too heavy to move inside, might ruin the new floors, so the Chief suggested we put him over there under the awnings. Should keep any rain off of him. We'll be moving the woman out of the townhouse tomorrow."

I looked at the canvased statue of Oswall. His outstretched hand poking out, forever trying to ward off his doom.

We left Webster to his task and went inside. As we passed Sergeant Constable Maginhart's desk, I snatched another biscuit from the tin. I had not eaten all day.

The kennel area was full of constables going about their business. It was a shift change, with a handful of them staying on for the night. Crime never sleeps.

"Chief's here," Fairfax said, and I saw the rock lights in his office were on.

As we entered the Chief saw me, stood and rounded his large desk. He took my hand into both of his, and for the briefest of moments, I thought he would kiss it. Now wouldn't that have been a thrill at my age?

"Beeweather!" Chief Constable Kyrill said. "Such a pleasure to see you again. I do wish it was under different circumstances though. How are you feeling?" He noticed how tired I was.

"I'm fine, thank you," I said. I blushed at his attention. "It has been a rather long day."

Kyrill released my hand and motioned to a chair. "Please sit," he said, and I did. It felt good to relax a little but my mind was still heavy with thoughts of the case.

Kyrill looked to Fairfax, "So, any progress?"

Fairfax opened his mouth to answer when a voice from the doorway behind us cut him off.

"That is what I want to know!" It was Sigwald Archambault looking flush from hurrying through the kennel to confront us.

Behind him arrived his lick-spittle of an assistant, Davlon Blythe. Upon seeing me, Blythe sneered, which only emphasized the ugly birthmark under his left eye.

"Mister Mayor," the Chief said with a sigh. "To what do we owe this interruption?" He had no admiration for Archambault, of which I was grateful. It would only make the lives of the entire Constabulary that much more difficult.

Archambault glared at me. "What is she still doing on the case? I made it perfectly clear that reactivating retired personnel was against regulations unless approved through a committee -".

Kyrill stopped him with a raised hand, annoyance on his face. "Enough Sigwald. We know why you are really here. You are sore at Beeweather for throwing your crooked business partners into a deep, dark hole. And now you see an opportunity to vent your spleen."

Archambault's face was near apoplectic. "How dare you make such a vile accusation, sir! My concern is only that the rules are followed. Allowing an old woman to trollop through a very important case with her little animal show is not one of them!"

Blythe sniffed approval at his master's tirade.

Kyrill took a step closer to the mayor, looming over the smaller man. "Who I assign to a case is my responsibility. Not yours. If you wish to file a formal complaint then please do."

"I will!" said the mayor, wide eyed.

"Although," the Chief said, "it would be a complete waste of time as the case will most likely be solved by then."

The mayor's eyes bounced between the Chief and myself as if looking for a hint of deception. "Is this true? Do you have a suspect?"

I spoke for myself. "We have leads, but I believe we will have something soon." That might not have been true, but if felt good to say it to the mayor.

Fairfax leaned forward. "And most all the progress we made today was thanks to her little animal show."

Archambault's eyes glanced at my satchel and, for a moment, he looked worried. He turned to Chief Kyrill. "Then this time tomorrow, Chief Constable, if a suspect is not in custody, I will have your badge."

Chief Kyrill blinked in surprise. But before he could respond in kind, Archambault whirled around and marched out the office, with Blythe scurrying close behind.

Once the two were out of earshot everyone in the office let out a sigh of relief.

"What an unpleasant little man," I said, not for the first time that day.

"No matter how many times he is reelected," Chief Kyrill said, "his manners never improve."

Fairfax said, "Can he do that, sir? Just take your badge away on such a whim?"

The Chief shrugged, "Perhaps. But not without a fight from the Constabulary's supporters on the council, few they may be. Oh, he'll raise a stink and make life a little more difficult, but he's been doing that for years, anyway." He looked hopeful for a moment. "Do you have a lead?"

I looked to Fairfax who could only offer a supportive smile. "Well, Chief Constable, we are working on that as hard as we can."

Kyrill raised a hand. "That is all I ask for. But for now, I think you two should get some rest. You both look drained."

"Yes, sir," said Fairfax. "Thank you, sir."

As we left the Chief's office and went back to the buggy, a sensation of cold dread washed over me. There was more at stake here than an old detective's professional pride.

If I could not close this case and the Chief was replaced with a puppet of the mayor, then the entire future of the Constabulary would be at risk.

CHAPTER TWELVE

After Fairfax dropped me off at my home, I immediately went to the kitchen and made myself a cheese and beet sandwich. A favorite of mine since childhood, I found some small solace in the ritual of eating it. The taste was wonderful.

As I ate, my eyes wandered to my satchel which sat open on the kitchen chair beside me. Next to the knitting bag was my little pistol. I took it out and, not for the first time that day, checked to ensure it was loaded.

I wondered at such an odd life I had led. To be at such a stage in my later years that a pistol was required for my safety. When was it fired last? During the case of the wolfmen pack that stalked the Hearts district? No. During the case of the demon which took over the King of the Rats? No, that was too far back in the past.

As I tried to conjure the memory, I yawned. Such things were best to not think of before bed. It would only create nightmares, and of those I already had plenty. I put the pistol on the table and looked at how the rock lights played across its steel surface. I hoped before this case was over, I would not need to use it.

Tired, I picked up my satchel and went to my bedroom, turning off the rock lights along the way. I readied for bed, and as I climbed in I looked at the knitting bag in the satchel on the night stand. Now that brought back memories. Strong and fierce. My old mind did not need coaxing for those.

I turned off the rock light by my bed and closed my eyes. Sleep claimed me quickly and the vision of Oswall being lowered by the crane haunted my dreams.

xxx

I woke with a start and sat upright in bed.

My heart thumped in my chest as my eyes searched the darkness for what yanked me from my slumber. Was it a noise, or a nightmare?

The room was pitch black, but I resisted the urge to touch a rock light. I had lived in this house for decades and I knew all of its creaks and pops when its old wood shifted. Now I listened. I sensed something was wrong.

Then it came. A slight creaking of the floorboard at the end of the hall that bordered the kitchen.

Someone was in the house.

My mind raced with the implications. No one had broken into my house before. I had taken precautions. Yet, with another creaking noise, this one closer, the fact was undeniable.

I fought down the panic that threatened to overwhelm me. I was, after all, a little old woman who lived alone. But this old woman had bite!

I realized I had an advantage, albeit temporary. I knew this house very well; the perpetrator did not. Also, based on how he or she moved, they were unaware I had woken. I could prepare for them.

In the darkness, I eased across my bed until I was up against the night stand. I reached over to my satchel and placed my hand inside, searching. Where was my pistol? Then it hit me. Like a fool, I had left it on the kitchen table. Maybe the person skulking in my hallway had it in their possession and sought to shoot me with it. How fitting.

Cursing inwardly, I tried to think. There was my rifle in the closet next to the night stand, loaded but stuffed behind a bunch of clothing. Not very helpful, yet I had little choice.

I moved off the bed and placed a foot on the cold floor. The wood beneath my foot crackled loudly.

Suddenly, the intruder gave up all pretense of stealth and rushed down the hall.

I lunged for the closet door in a last desperate gamble to grab the rifle, but I knew I would be too late. I slipped and in my effort to maintain balance I lashed out with one hand. My fingers grazed the rock light on the night stand and it flicked on. I bumped against it as I fell to the floor. The light flung across the room to land spinning at the bedroom doorway.

The rock light spun, casting swirling shadows and light around the room. Then I saw him. A man, tall and lean, covered in black clothing. His face was covered with a black mask but his eyes were wide with anger. He held a pistol in his hand.

I gasped and reached up to right myself. If I was going to die, it would be on my feet.

The man entered the room and kicked the spinning rock light to the side. Its dim illumination cast him almost completely in shadow, and his eyes flickered like hateful jewels.

I stood, but my old body defied me one last fight and I sagged backward. My hand landed in my satchel and that's when I touched the knitting bag's clasp.

What happened next was nothing short of miraculous.

A cat leapt from the knitting bag and it was unlike any I had seen previously. It was a mottled gray color and absolutely huge. One instance, the bag was open, and the next, a cat the size of a small horse stood in the space between myself and the man in black.

The gigantic cat arched its back, long fur standing on end, and hissed so loud the sound shook the house.

Stunned, the man in black froze, eyes wide in shock. He fired his pistol, and I flinched at the sound. The man backpedaled and raced back down the hallway.

The cat ran after him, or so it tried. Due to its size and the slippery nature of the floor, the giant cat slid into the door frame, cracking it. A painting flew from the wall with the impact.

I heard the man keening with fear as he fled, neither yelling nor screaming, but a sound of utter terror.

The cat's claws scraped at the floor as it scrambled to get proper purchase and give pursuit. It soon vanished from sight, thudding against a wall out in the hall.

I gathered my wits, hurried to the closet and pulled out the rifle. In the kitchen, I heard the back door being flung open with a load crash. I hobbled into the hallway, my side hurting from my fall.

I saw the open back door and the blackness of night beyond it. The huge cat stood at the edge of the door hissing into the night, but it would not step over into the back yard. The man had fled.

Once I made it to the kitchen I headed for the open door. The large feline whirled around and hissed at me. I froze. Had the beast become so fired up from the attack that it might hurt me?

I realized the meaning of its consternation. The one true limit of these cats was if summoned from within a building or domicile, they were then bound to that place. This cat could not go outside. Had it been summoned outside, there would have been no such limitation and I do not doubt it would still be chasing after the petrified man.

And since going outside was not an option, it could not protect me if I left. Which is why it now refused to let me pass. Touched as I was by its sentiments, I found myself a little annoyed. I had looked forward to firing a shot at the black-hearted cretin who defiled my home and tried to murder me in my sleep.

The cat paced back and forth at the open door, agitated. I took the moment to touch several rock lights and assess my situation.

I was safe now, at least for the moment. Whoever had broken in would not be foolish enough to return. I was wide awake, armed and angry. And now, accompanied by my horse sized guardian, I doubted another attempt would be made on me that night.

To the cat, I said, "I'd like to shut the door. It's letting in a draft."

The giant feline paused and regarded me. With a swish of its long bushy tail, the door slammed shut and the dead bolt slide into place, locked.

I then realized it had been shot when the man fired the pistol. "Are you all right? I thought he might have hit you." I saw no obvious wounds and it did not act as if hurt.

The large animal began to wretch as if to cough up a fur-ball. And for a cat that size it would have been quite the sight. Instead, something small fell from its mouth to clatter on the floor. With a cloth from the kitchen, I picked it up. A small caliber bullet, and still perfectly formed. Almost as if it had been absorbed intact.

I looked to the cat in amazement. It stared back with rainbow eyes then resumed its march back and forth.

I thought it wise to avoid the windows for the rest of the night on the off chance the man may try to shoot at me from the dark. Paranoia, I know. But considering someone just tried to kill me, I allowed for the safe guard.

Snatching my pistol off the kitchen table, I went into the sitting room which I kept it in complete dark. I sat in the big easy chair in the far corner. From here, I would detect if the intruder returned. And I'd be ready.

The cat paced up and down the hallway, making stressful warbling noises. Soon, it calmed a little and padded over. The large feline flopped onto the rug at my feet and stretched out.

I contemplated going up the lane to the Elderbright's residence, who had a phone, to call the Constabulary. But that would have required me getting dressed and stumbling around the dark with a potential murderer skulking in the trees. And I did not think my new friend would have any of that nonsense.

With the loaded rifle across my lap I fought against my tired body and waited for the morning sun.

CHAPTER THIRTEEN

I woke to the sound of knocking at my front door.

Bleary-eyed, I looked around the room. My large guardian was gone. Apparently satisfied that my safety was not in question, it had returned to the knitting bag. I stood with an audible creak from my bones and waddled to the front door. With the rifle at the ready, I opened it.

Fairfax was standing there, smiling and holding a tin of biscuits. The smile vanished when he saw my state and the rifle in my hands.

"By the Gods, Mayra! What happened? Are you all right?"

I waved a dismissive hand, but was still touched by his concern. "Nothing an old woman like me couldn't handle, along with the help of an immense cat."

At his confused expression, I chuckled. "I'm okay, Fairfax, I promise."

As I told him what happened, his face became more and more grim. When I finished, Fairfax did not match my gaze. This appeared to affect him more than it did me.

He said, "You should have called the Constabulary. I would have come right away."

"Agreed. But I had little choice, didn't I? Come now, let's go inside and I can put on proper detective clothing. Morning wear doesn't help with interrogations."

While I dressed in the bedroom, Fairfax paced around the house, checking and rechecking the latches on the windows and grumbling to himself. He even walked the perimeter of the yard looking at every leaf and blade of grass.

Once I was ready, I emerged with my satchel over a shoulder and met him outside.

"Let us check the woods further back," Fairfax said. "He may have left tracks or something of note."

I would have pointed out such an effort was useless but acquiesced. He was upset he had not been present to protect me. For that, I could entertain a short jaunt through the woods. "Very, well, Constable," I said with a smile. "Lead the way."

My property bordered a nature preserve which was a polite way to describe land that no one wanted to buy. Thick with trees and underbrush, it had thwarted my last adventurous attempts to hike through it. Instead, I went to the park a few minutes away. This time, the forest did not yield its secrets any easier than before.

After several minutes, I lost my patience. "Fairfax, I do not think we will find anything in this mess. Let us return."

"Just a little further," Fairfax said, soldiering on. It was as if the branches and brambles did not exist to him, pushing through relentlessly. I wondered if I should be concerned. Was this more than hurt pride?

Fairfax stopped and crouched. "There," he said in a hushed voice. "Up ahead. Do you see?"

I tottered up beside him and put a hand on his broad shoulder to steady myself on the uneven ground. Looking where he pointed, I saw a cave or entranceway in a hillside.

"Let us take a closer look," Fairfax said and moved forward, pistol in hand.

"What if there is a bear?" I said, taking my pistol out of the satchel.

"Then you can summon a bear-eating cat," Fairfax said, and I caught the profile of a grin on his face.

We approached at an angle to get a better look. Then Fairfax stood straight and frowned. "It's a sewer grate."

The round cave contained the concrete workings of a sewage tunnel entrance. A large grate barred any access. A foul smelling trickle of water seeped out of it and into the ground.

"Well," I said. "That was anticlimactic."

A huge old padlock was secured to the grate. Fairfax pointed at it. "Can one of your friends do something with this?"

"What? And go prancing through the sewers? I don't think so, Fairfax." But at his expression I sighed and looked at the knitting bag's clasp. It was wooden. "Sorry," I said. "They do not want to come out to play."

Fairfax looked at the muddy ground just outside the concrete entrance. "No boot marks. There are animal tracks but little else." He stood and glowered at the sewer grate. "I'm willing to bet he came through this."

I shrugged. "Maybe he did. But I will admit it is good to know that this thing is here. And perhaps a little disconcerting." Very disconcerting. A secret highway for robbers and thugs that spits out onto my backyard. I wondered how extensive the sewer network was.

"Okay," Fairfax said. "Let's return, shall we?"

As we shuffled back to the house Fairfax asked, "He tried to shoot at you with a pistol. But the cat blocked it. Right?"

"Yes, that's right," I wheezed. This hiking was for younger people, that was a certainty.

"Why didn't he try to turn you to stone with the Talon? Why switch to a pistol now?"

That was a good question and one I had not considered. After a few moments thought, I said, "Most artifacts and relics need time to recharge their magic. My guess is the Talon was not ready to be used again, hence the pistol."

Fairfax said, "Then, based on the rough time frames when Elicia and Oswall were stoned, maybe it can only be used once a day. Or after a long stretch of hours."

"Sounds reasonable, Fairfax, but we cannot know for certain. We should consider it usable at any time."

At the buggy we took a rest. I leaned against the hood and panted like an old hound dog returning from a hunt.

"Where to this morning?" Fairfax said as he eyed our surroundings.

"I had time to mull things over last night," I said. "There is a definite connection between the museum burglary and Elicia."

"And what is that?"

"Not a what. A who," I said, opening the buggy's passenger door. "Come, Fairfax. We have one more interview which may finally result in a solid lead."

xxx

A fog had fallen across the Hearts District making driving more of a chore. But we located the Hubertus residence after I convinced Fairfax to stop and ask for directions from a roadside clockworks toy seller.

The Hubertus home was a narrow townhouse quite like Elicia's, only theirs was painted a bright yellow from ground to roof. Pasha Hubertus was no doubt responsible for the choice in color.

"My eyes hurt if I look at it too long," Fairfax said as we parked and got out.

"We need to be on our best behavior with these two," I said as we climbed the stairs. "There are questions that may put an end to this, and they have the answers. So, if asked, you love the color."

Fairfax sighed and followed.

The moment I rapped on the door it flew open. Pasha stood in the doorway, a flummoxed look on her face. She had forgone blue for today and instead wore an outfit of eye-shattering green.

"This cannot be good," Pasha said. Her eyes darted between Fairfax and I.

"Mrs. Hubertus, we have follow-up questions for you and your husband. Is Mr. Hubertus here?" I said.

For a moment Pasha appeared to be trying to decide on whether to slam the door. Instead, she turned her head and bellowed, "Win! Those coppers are back!"

"Who?" Winimar called from the bowels of the house.

"Coppers!" She looked at us, eyes contorted with suspicion.

"Well, ask them in for tea!" Winimar said.

Pasha's stern expression transformed into a bright and happy smile. "We've put tea on. Would you like some?"

This woman runs hot and cold, I thought. Her husband must be perpetually scatter-shot.

I thanked her and we entered the tiny foyer. After slamming the door, Pasha led us through a hall into a kitchen. Winimar was sitting at a table, hunched over a newspaper.

As we entered, he said, "Looking for a new job. These want ads are for the dogs."

Pasha waved at the table for us to take a chair. I sat but Fairfax opted to stand to one side of me. He was on his guard and was ready to draw his pistol in an instant. I had told him I was uncertain whether the Hubertus couple had anything to do with the murders. How they answered my questions would decide that.

Winimar pointed at the newspaper. "The only jobs in here worth looking at are for people with clockwork skills. That's not for me. I have enough trouble attaching rock lights to their clamps, let alone messing with little gears and pulleys."

"Your fingers are too fat, Win," Pasha said as she prepared tea at the counter. I kept an eye on what her hands were doing.

"Maybe I'll just shovel coal," Winimar said. "Always need people to do that. Don't last long on the job, but at least it pays."

I offered a commiserating smile. "Mr. Hubertus, I was wondering if you could tell us how you got the job at the High Garden Museum?"

Pasha caused a small clatter with the dishes.

Winimar said, "Oh, yes. That was a bit of luck on my part, really. Didn't even need to look through the paper. It sort of landed in my lap."

When he did not elaborate, I asked, "Yes, but how? Was it offered to you or did you apply?"

Pasha turned, her tea task forgotten. "What does that have to do with anything? What's it matter how someone got a job?"

Winimar looked surprised at Pasha's outburst. "Pash, dear. It's okay." He looked at me. "Turns out, I have a family connection with favors he could call on. Really high up in the government. Makes things so much easier for a little fellow like me when you know someone, well, in the know."

"A family connection with the museum?" I said.

"Well, not the museum. He just has influence enough in town that he can get things done with little bother."

"Who is this family connection?"

"My cousin," Winimar said. "He knew I was out of work, having lost my job with the sewage department, due to them closing down large sections of the tunnels. And like an angel, he appeared and said he had the perfect job for me. At the museum. Never been there in my life, have I Pash? And yet the very next day, I was on the job, making rounds and earning a salary better than the sewage department could ever offer."

I casually slid my hand into my satchel. "And who is your cousin, exactly?"

He looked between myself and Fairfax as if the answer was obvious. "Why, his name's Davlon. Davlon Blythe."

A volcano of emotion surged within me, roiling through my body and threatened to explode. I heard Fairfax grind his teeth.

Winimar, for his sake, looked baffled at our reaction. "Don't you know him? Works for Mayor Archambault, he does. His right-hand man."

I made a tremendous effort not to scream. Instead, I took a breath and asked, "Once you were working at the museum did Mr. Blythe ask you for any favors in return?"

"Just one," Winimar said. "And it wasn't a very big favor either, if you ask me. He only wanted me to tell him when new objects and things arrived from the Capital. Figured I'd be the first to know since I had the run of the place."

When neither I nor Fairfax said anything more, Winimar looked worried. "Am I in more trouble now?"

Pasha swatted her husband with a spoon and said, "Told you this would be no good."

CHAPTER FOURTEEN

Erring on the side of caution, we brought both Winimar and Pasha to the Constabulary to be held for further questioning as a pretext. I did not think there was much else they might offer in the way of information, but it kept them from warning Blythe that we were looking for him.

Once the Hubertus couple were tucked away, Fairfax and I drove straight to the mayor's offices located at the Town Hall.

"Should we confront him directly?" Fairfax asked. He was eager to collar Blythe.

"Let's give it a few hours, I want to watch him and see what he does," I said. "We might learn something. When Winimar and Pasha are released we can question him.

Fairfax glowered. "We still have no direct evidence to him and the killings. Not unless he has the Talon on his person or spits out an admission of guilt."

I didn't disagree. What little we had to hang on Blythe was minor to the point of being laughable. Yet, I still wanted a chance to observe the man, now he was our prime suspect.

The plan was to stake out the mayor's office from a distance and follow Blythe when he left. But when we arrived at the Town Hall, the place was locked. There was no sign of the mayor's big white car which meant Blythe was driving it around somewhere at that moment.

Fairfax stopped the buggy next to a gardener tending to the bushes next to the building and asked him why it was closed.

"Strangest thing," the gardener said, wiping sweat from his brow. "Mayor declared today a holiday. Told everyone to go home. Not me though, I chose to stay 'cause work still needs to get done, holiday or not."

"Holiday for what?" I asked.

The gardener shrugged. "Beats me, ma'am. Said that there would be a grand spectacle, later today. A once in a lifetime event. Everyone should prepare themselves, he said. Sounds loopy to me. But the mayor has always been off kilter."

I asked, "Do you know if the mayor's assistant is still inside?"

"You missed him. Drove off with the mayor a short while ago in that huge white buggy of his."

"Know where they went?"

"Sorry, not a clue. Hopefully they went to find a new mayor."

We thanked the gardener and drove on.

"Now where?" Fairfax asked.

"Let's try the mayor's house as a start. We may get lucky."

The mayor maintained a residence in White Cliff, a rich part of town. Fairfax knew of the mayor's mansion and took us there.

As we drove, I touched on the facts of the case. "So Blythe uses his connections to put Winimar on the payroll of the museum. Blythe manipulates him to give information on the items arriving. He learns of Gunther's Stone Talon this way and gains access to the museum. Blythe then casts a sleep spell on Winimar, opens the vault - probably with another spell - and takes the trunk with the Talon in it."

Fairfax said, "Spells Winimar to sleep but doesn't kill him. Why?"

I shrugged. "In regards to family, Blythe might have a conscience. So he has the Talon but can't use it. He becomes aware of the Mad Scribe's book with the reversal spell in it. At first, he tries to buy it from Rousset."

"While wearing women's make-up," Fairfax said with a shake of his head.

"True. A bad disguise, but it was to cover his birthmark which would have made him easy to identify with Rousset's description."

Fairfax coughed a laugh. "That is an awful disguise if you consider it."

"Yes, but it kept us from making a direct connection to him," I said.

"Here it is," Fairfax said as we drove past a large beautiful mansion. A driveway pulled up to the front doors with the huge white buggy parked out front. We kept on going.

"At least they are there," Fairfax said. "I'll park up ahead and try and get an angle on the place."

Thankfully, the mayor's mansion was near the base of a hill. We drove up the hill, turned around and parked. From our vantage point, we could see most of the building.

After a few minutes of no activity below, I continued with my fact list. "Unable to purchase the book Blythe then approaches Elicia with the promise of money if she would steal it from the shop. She does, and he uses its spell to reactivate the Talon, binds it to himself and turn her to stone."

"And Oswall?"

"Well, by this time Oswall had quizzed Pasha Hubertus about Winimar's job while the man was asleep. Pasha must have revealed Winimar got the job because of Blythe. Sensing a potential angle, Oswall then followed Blythe around which takes him to Rousset's store. After Blythe leaves, perhaps the next day, Oswall went in to talk to Rousset but he was at the auction. Oswall talks with Elicia, what is said I can only guess. In regards to Blythe's earlier visit or, as you say, he was looking for a date."

Fairfax said, "Elicia probably mentioned Oswall to Blythe. She'd have been anxious as she just stolen the book or was going to."

"Yes, when Blythe learns Oswall had spoken to Elicia, he panics," I said. "So Blythe calls into the Constabulary and anonymously tells Oswall that he has information about the burglary, and to meet at the bridge at Muddy Shore."

"And there Blythe turns him to stone."

I nodded. "And he even had the gall to return to the scene while we were there surveying it."

Fairfax scowled. "And then to come to the Constabulary later on."

"To sneer at us," I said. The hot flush of anger sparked in my gut.

"Well, when I get my hands on him, he'll wish -" Fairfax said before I interrupted with a shout.

"There he is!" I pointed.

Sure enough, Davon Blythe had exited the rear of the mansion and was making his way along a path into the forest which crowded around the property.

"What the devil is he doing?"

We watched as he vanished into the woods.

"He's leaving is what he is doing," I said and opened the buggy door. "Quick, we mustn't lose him!"

Fairfax did not argue the point and got out.

"How do we follow him without announcing our presence?" I asked, looking at the terrain.

Fairfax said. "The trees are thick here. Let's try to approach from this way."

I grumbled, but did not protest. We stumped our way through the foliage. After a few minutes I started to worry. "Two nature hikes in one day. How are we going to find him in this?"

At that moment, we broke through the forest to look down on a small valley. And there, clear as day, was Blythe walking along a path at its bottom.

Fairfax crouched and pulled me down with him.

Blythe walked up to a cave with a grate across it. No, not a cave, I realized. A sewer entrance. Blythe took out a set of keys and unlocked a padlock on the grate. He looked around to see if he was being followed.

Fairfax pulled me down lower, which was a near physical impossibility at this point.

Blythe then opened the grate, entered and closed it behind him.

"Winimar worked for the sewage department. Blythe must have gotten those keys from him."

"The same sewers that lead to your back yard," Fairfax said. "I'm up for a trip through the sewers. What about you?"

"If it helps us put an end to this monster, I'd swim through the sewers of Hades itself," I said.

"I'll take that as a yes," Fairfax said, and we descended to the valley bottom.

We came up to the grate and peered inside. Only a yawning darkness could be seen. Fairfax pointed at the padlock. "Do you think they will help this time?"

I checked inside my satchel. The clasp was wooden. "No, not this time. Perhaps we should -" I said, but stopped as Fairfax picked up a large rock.

"What are you doing?" I said.

"This," Fairfax said and hit the padlock with the rock. The lock shattered.

I sighed. "You realize that not only are we trespassing on private property, but you just committed breaking and entering?" I don't know why I felt the need to tease him at that moment.

Fairfax dropped the rock and clapped his hands clean. "I'll be sure to bring up those points with the Chief during my next review." He grinned. "Now please tell me you brought rock lights."

For a moment, I considering lying and turning us back, but Blythe was so close now. He had to be stopped if for no other reason than to keep him from turning another victim to stone.

"Yes," I said. "I came prepared." I dug through my satchel and pulled out two small rock lights and gave one to Fairfax. They winked on at our touch.

Fairfax pushed the grate open and produced his pistol. I did the same with mine.

"Are you ready?"

"Always," I said. But I was not sure I meant it.
We entered the sewers.

CHAPTER FIFTEEN

The tunnel which led from the entrance was long and winding. If not for the rock lights in our hands, we would have been in total darkness. Our footsteps and breathing echoed against the concrete.

I was thankful there had been no rain that day or we would have been up to our knees in water and filth. Now the water was just a narrow trickle under our feet.

"How far does this go?" I asked. My legs ached, and I cursed my old bones.

Fairfax pointed, "There is a junction ahead." He looked at me concerned. "Do you need help?" He offered an arm.

I waved him away. "I'm fine. Just not keen on dark cramped places."

The tunnel ended in a T-junction with branches going left and right. And there before us was a huge engraving on the wall.

"The Mark of Quantiqtl," Fairfax said.

It was greater in height than Fairfax and more detailed than the others we had seen. Its long tentacles outstretched with an opened beak-like mouth between them.

"Well, Constable," I said. "I believe we are on the right track."

"Yes, but which way?"

I peered in both directions. A faint light could be seen further down the right one. "I see something, Fairfax. This way."

We walked toward the far light. As we got closer the light became bright enough to douse our own rock lights.

The tunnel ended at a wide archway, and beyond it appeared to be a chamber. Fairfax motioned me to stop, and tip-toed ahead. Hugging the wall, he peered through the archway.

He turned to me and shrugged. "No one there," he said in a hushed voice. Mindful of potential danger, we stepped through.

The chamber was huge with dozens of rock lights ensconced along the walls. The ceiling so high it could not be seen.

Fairfax looked to our left and let out a surprised shout. I looked, too, and my breath caught in my throat.

A large statue of a squid sat at one side of the chamber. It stood more than three times the height of a horse and was as wide as my house. Long stone tentacles reached outward in a frozen roiling mass as if searching for food. Two large, sightless eyes seemed to glare at us, angry and wild. The bulk of its body extended behind it like a train car.

"Quantiqtl," I said.

Fairfax and I stared in amazement. The bright rock lights enhancing its shadows making it appear almost alive.

"Incredible work," Fairfax said. "It must have taken years to carve."

A thought hit me which sent shivers down my spine. Wide-eyed, I grabbed Fairfax's arm and pulled him backward, away from the statue.

"That is not just any statue, Fairfax," I said as the full horror of realization struck home.

"That is the smartest thing you have ever said," came a loud voice from behind us. We whirled around, pistols at the ready.

Sigwald Archambault and Davlon Blythe emerged from a side entrance. Both wore black robes with the Mark of Quantiqtl on their sleeves. Blythe pointed a pistol at us. Archambault held what looked to be a long narrow bone sharpened to a point. I realized it was the Talon.

"Mr. Mayor," I said with dripping sarcasm. "Why am I not surprised you are behind this?"

"Retired Detective Beeweather," Archambault said, returning the sarcasm. "Of course I am behind this. Who else can bring about the dawning of a new era?"

I regarded Blythe, who sneered. To him, I said, "So Davlon, the responsibility of wielding the Talon was too much for you? You shifted the binding over to Sigwald because you lacked the courage to keep using it?"

Blythe's sneer turned to anger. "He is the chosen one! I am but a tool for him to wield on his journey to rebuild the world."

"You are most certainly a tool," Fairfax said.

"Shut up!" Barked Archambault. He waved the Talon around. "Blythe did as commanded. He follows the same calling as me in our service to the one great god. And soon, we will all serve him, or perish."

I glanced at the huge tentacled statue. "You mean -", I said before Archambault cut me off.

"Do not speak of the great one while in his presence! You are unworthy of such an honor."

Fairfax said, "What do you mean in his presence?"

Keeping my pistol aimed at the mayor, I said, "That statue *is* the Quantiqtl. The real one from long ago. Turned to stone by Gunther."

Fairfax blanched at the implications.

Archambault grinned. "Yes, now you realize the true import of what I am trying to accomplish. This is the great and mighty Quantiqtl! Betrayed in battle by that ungrateful wretch, Gunther. But soon his crime will be corrected and the entire world will rejoice!"

"This raving lunatic is boring me," Fairfax said. "Can I shoot him now?"

My curiosity got the better of me and I asked, "What is it you think you can do?" Asking questions of the mayor fed his giant ego and might buy me time to devise a plan.

Archambault's eyes widened, and he smiled. "Why, to resurrect the Great One and restore him to his rightful place as the ruler of the universe!"

My eyes went to the Talon in his hand. Again, I was struck with a terrifying realization. "You've used the spell from the book to reverse the Stone casting ability of the Talon," I said. It was a statement and one that chilled me.

Archambault laughed. "Now you know, foolish woman! Yes, and I will undo the Stoning of the Ancient One and return him to life! And our mighty god will reward me beyond my wildest dreams!"

I arched a brow at these two idiots. "If you cannot use the Talon to turn one of us to stone then it's no threat to us. So it is our two pistols to Blythe's one."

Archambault's reverie faltered. He seemed to realize that the situation was not as much to his favor as his ravings had led him to believe.

Blythe tensed, his pistol moving between me and Fairfax.

My pistol remained on Archambault. He could not be allowed to use the Talon. Not for what he intended to do. "Drop the Talon, Sigwald. Otherwise, I will be forced to shoot."

Archambault's face contorted in an expression caught between sanity and servitude to his chosen God. In an instant he made his decision.

The mayor turned the Talon toward the huge statue. I fired my pistol, hitting the mayor in the shoulder. But as I did so, Blythe fired at me with a scream of rage.

At that moment, Fairfax jumped in front of me, grunted in pain and knocked me down.

A loud and terrifying roar shattered the air causing the chamber walls to vibrate. I looked knowing full well what I would see, but did not want to.

Quantiqtl was alive. The huge squid raged and thrashed its long tentacles about smashing against the rocky chamber's walls. The impact shook the room and a loud cracking was heard above us.

I grasped at Fairfax to see if he was alive. He groaned in pain but looked at me with concern. "Winged me, the lucky grubber!" he said to my relief.

Archambault lay on the ground clutching his wounded shoulder, but he did not care. His face was one of reverence as he looked at Quantiqtl.

Blythe had lowered his pistol and stood in a dazed stupor, eyes locked on his now-living God.

Quantiqtl roared again and pulled itself closer to us. The motion of something so huge and frightening paralysed me with fear. Man was not meant to gaze on such evil and stay lucid.

The beast flailed wildly and hit the walls again.

This time, the ceiling high above cracked even louder. Huge chunks of concrete and stone fell from above.

"Look out!" Fairfax cried and threw himself over top of me. The noise of the crumbling ceiling was deafening. Within a few moments it subsided and Fairfax and I looked.

Thick dust choked the air and a large mound of rubble now took up most of the chamber. Blythe and Archambault had been under the falling rocks and were buried.

The collapse only agitated the Ancient One even more, and it pulled itself forward, huge eyes locked on us. A tentacle lashed out at me and Fairfax moved in its way.

The large man was cast aside like a toy and landed in a heap on the other side of the chamber.

"Fairfax!" I cried. As I tried to stand up to go to him, the squid moved closer and shrieked, its beaked mouth opening wide showing rows of sharp teeth.

For a moment, I was transfixed by the great being, and the sight of the surrounding carnage. The creature pulled itself forward again and raised its vast tentacles, preparing to put an end to me.

I did the only thing I could think of in that terrifying moment. I reached into my satchel and touched the knitting bag's clasp.

A cat jumped out of the bag. Then another. Followed by another. And another. Soon, cats poured out of the bag like water from a hydrant. Dozens, then hundreds and even thousands. Each flying out with such an amazing speed they blurred past my vision.

Quantiqtl shrieked in confusion and retreated. Cats flew through the air, ran along the ground, and swirled around the giant squid like a feline maelstrom. When the Ancient One thrashed out its tentacles the cats avoided them then resumed their assault.

Stunned, there was nothing I could do but stare. So many magical cats in one place. I had never seen more than one at a time, now it appeared to be a near infinite number of them. And they were all here to aid me.

I smiled.

The torrent of cats from the bag suddenly ended, and I looked at its dark opening. It was pitch black within, a void without limits.

Then a paw emerged, and another. With calm purpose a cat pulled itself out of the bag.

This cat was unlike any other. It wasn't one color. It was every color. From its flat snout to the end of its long bushy tail, its fur was a vibrant rainbow of multicolored hues. It turned its head to look at me. Its eyes did not have irises and were completely white which glowed with an inner energy.

I stared in amazement at this incredible creature. No, not creature. This being was far more than that.

"Hello," I said.

The cat blinked at me and from within its eyes I sensed an old soul, older than anything I'd ever encountered before, or ever would. And I realized at that moment what this cat was.

Quantiqtl's roars now turned to shrieks of fear. It did not know how to deal with this enemy.

The cat then turned from me and sauntered over to the rubble under which Archambault was buried. On the rock strewn floor rested the Talon. With its mouth the cat picked it up, then walked over to me. It sat down, looked at me, and waited.

Its eyes spoke to me, at a place deep within my soul. There was a magic there I could not hope to fathom. But I knew then what it wanted me to do.

I took the Talon from its mouth, and felt its binding shift to me. I pointed it at Quantiqtl.

The great squid must have sensed what was about to happen and roared in defiance, one last time.

Guided by the inner whispers of the special cat, I called for a magical incantation from a secret place within my soul.

Quantiqtl shrieks ended in an instant. The Ancient One was turned to stone once again.

The swirl of a thousand cats subsided and each flew to the knitting bag to stream back inside. As they zipped past my face, I caught the multicolored cat sitting and staring at me with its glowing white eyes. I knew how special this encounter was and it filled my heart with joy.

When the last cat vanished back into its home, the multicolored feline stood. It regarded the stoned version of Quantiqtl. Then it made a light sneezing noise.

The huge stone Quantiqtl shattered, and crumbled into a million pieces. The remains looked no different than the rock and concrete which filled the chamber.

The cat then walked over to the knitting bag and, without a goodbye look, it was gone.

My heart beat against my chest for I knew what that cat really was: an Ancient One.

From behind me I heard a groan.

"Fairfax!" I cried and hobbled over to him.

He was missing his cap and his hair was tussled. He leaned up and rubbed at his head. I saw his arm was bleeding from a bullet wound.

"Are you okay?" I was worried for him, perhaps in more ways than I wanted to admit.

He blinked at me and said, "I think it knocked some sense into me." He smiled, and I nearly fainted with relief.

"Can you walk?" I asked.

"I'll walk out of here," he said, pulling himself up to his feet favoring his left arm. He looked around. "Took care of it, did you?"

I laughed. "Well, I had help."

"Let me guess. Your animal circus made an appearance."

"You have no idea. I'm now of the firm belief that there is no such thing as too many cats! Let's get out of here and fix you up."

"There is no real fix for me, Mayra," he said. "I am who I am after all."

"I wouldn't have you any other way," I said. And we hobbled back to the sewer tunnels.

CHAPTER SIXTEEN

I regarded the statues of Elicia Ipthorn and Radley Oswall beneath the awning of the back lot of the Constabulary. Elicia, sitting on her stone chair drinking from her stone teacup. Oswall, one hand outstretched, the other reaching for his pistol. A sense of excitement I had not felt for a long time filled my heart. In my hand, I held the Stone Talon. Bound to me now, with the help of the multicolored cat, or whatever that being was.

"You're going to have to rename that now," Fairfax said from beside me. One arm was in a sling and a mottled bruise on one side of his face. I found him to be as handsome as ever.

"How do you figure that?"

"Well, first it was Gunther's Stone Talon. Then it was Blythe's Stone Talon. Then it was Archambault's Stone Talon. So, Beeweather's Stone Talon? Does that have a good ring to it?"

I chuckled. "It is none of those, I'm happy to say. Once done, we'll give it back to the Capital Museum. They can name it whatever they like."

Constables crowded about the parking lot anxious to see what was about to happen.

Chief Constable Kyrill approached us. "Trying to decide which one should have the honor of going first?"

"Not at all," I said. "Ladies always go first."

I pointed the Talon at Elicia and, from a secret place within my soul, called forth the magical incantation.

And like a rock light being touched on, Elicia went from completely stone to completely real. She slurped at her tea for a moment before she realized where she was. Her eyes went wide and sputtered out her tea.

"What?" Elicia said. "What is this? Where am I?" She nearly fell out of her chair. "By the Gods!"

A pair of constables hurried to her side and gently guided her toward the Constabulary's back door. "What happened?" she said, before she disappeared inside.

"It will take her time to adjust. From her point of view she hasn't missed a few days. Only moments," Fairfax said.

I asked Chief Kyrill, "So, Rousset will not press charges for the book's theft?"

The Chief shook his head. "No, he thought being turned to stone was punishment enough. As for the book, it will be sent to the Capital Museum along with all the other items the mayor and Blythe had hoarded in their sewer lair."

"That was kind of him," I said, turning my attention to Oswall.

Fairfax asked, "You are certain this will work again so soon? Doesn't it need hours to recharge its magic?"

I grinned. "For this task, the Talon has been given a brief reprieve. Once Oswall is transformed it will go inert again." I thought of the Ancient cat and the unfathomable knowledge behind its glowing white eyes.

"It appears a lot of rules were broken for you," Fairfax said with a grin.

"Who else should the rules be broken for?" I said and pointed the Talon at Oswall.

As with Elicia, it was instantaneous. One moment solid stone, the next a real man, again.

Oswall was shouting, "No! Don't!" He pulled out his pistol.

"Stop Detective!" Chief Kyrill said. "Hold your fire! You are safe now!"

The detective, bewildered, was looking about in utter confusion. But he had the mind to holster his pistol much to everyone's relief.

"What the devil is going on?" Detective Oswall said.

"Allow me to explain inside, Detective," Chief Kyrill said as he led the confused man into the Constabulary.

My heart thumped with joy at the sight of him whole again.

Fairfax was smiling from ear to ear which stretched out his walrus mustache to comical proportions. "Now that business is taken care of." He held out a narrow little box, its lid open.

I frowned and glanced at the Talon. So much harm had been done with it. I hoped it would finally be put in a safe place back at the Capital.

With a thunk, I dropped it into the box which Fairfax snapped shut.

I said, "I just realized something. Remember when I put the case files on the ground and asked the cat to point out the one that led to Oswall's killer?"

"Yes," Fairfax said.

"Well, Oswall wasn't dead. Just transformed. So the cat did not move until I changed my wording from killer to attacker."

"Ah, very good," Fairfax said with a smile. "So, what now, Miss Beeweather? Another case, perhaps?" There was a glint in his eye.

I chuckled. "Not at all, Constable. Now I will take my leave. There are newspapers to be read and I am behind on them."

"Would you like me to drive you?"

I looked up at the morning sky, bright and happy. "No. I think I will walk, thank you. Spent too much time in dark, dank places. I need the light to help with my complexion."

I turned and walked toward the road.

Fairfax called after me, "What if we need your help on a case? Can I call on you?"

I turned and gave Fairfax my most mischievous grin. "You can call on me any time, Fairfax. But only on one condition."

"Name it."

"Next time," I said "bring biscuits." And with the satchel over my shoulder, I walked off into the morning sunshine.

END.